THE FUN PART

KYLIE GILMORE

The Fun Part: © 2025 by Kylie Gilmore

Cover design by: Sweet 'N Spicy Designs

Published by: Extra Fancy Books

ISBN-13: 978-1-64658-133-7

Kylie Gilmore® is a registered Trademark.

1

Mackenzie

My cousin and I engage in a small wrestling match. *Oof. Ow!* Hopefully no one witnesses this. We're standing right outside the venue of the Clover Park Valentine's Day dance in the freezing cold of a Connecticut winter.

Harper's fingers are like talons gripping my upper arms. I've got her by the upper arms, too, as we wiggle back and forth, fairly matched in strength and size.

If it weren't for these three-inch heels, I could take her.

She's blocking the door!

"Just listen!" Harper exclaims, twisting her arms out from under my grip and grabbing me by the shoulders.

"What!"

"How long has it been for you? Really."

I huff. This is her way of saying we should bail on the dance. I get her point, but it's too late to back out now. Her objection is that it's mostly family and friends we grew up with in there. Translation: no eligible single guys.

I shake off her grip. "Not relevant."

"Very relevant."

I pull my thin white coat tighter around me. "I'm freezing. Can we please go in?"

If brute strength doesn't work, try being polite. Good

manners are part of Lady 101, drilled into me since birth by my former-beauty-queen mom.

I narrow my eyes at Harper. This outfit isn't enough coverage for a prolonged outdoor wrestling match, but it was the only coat that looked right with my short red dress, which I had to wear to go with my metallic-red, strappy, spiked heels. The shoes were a Valentine's gift to myself.

I debate shoving her out of the way versus the risk of damage to my new heels. Harper's a fighter. Ask me how I know. We grew up together, born only three months apart. I'm the older, more mature one at twenty-six. Our dads are identical twins, so we resemble each other—medium height, straight brown hair, a nose that turns up a little at the end. Only I have blue eyes, and hers are hazel.

Harper shakes her head. "You need this more than I do. I had an awesome hookup two short months ago."

Brag, brag, brag. So what if it's been a teensy bit over eight months for me? I've been busy with work and stuff.

"We're not bailing," I insist. "Dad's restaurant catered it, and everyone's expecting us. It's Mason and May's engagement party, provided she said yes. And they could be here any minute!"

She gives me a hard look, which I return, setting my jaw in determination. It's too late to back out, and no way am I showing up single to a couples' event without her. I've been a single bridesmaid at enough weddings to know my limits.

She lets out an exasperated sigh. "Don't you want to meet someone tall, dark, and handsome?"

I scoff. "Tall, dark, and handsome? You've been watching too many old black-and-white movies." This is a new thing with her. I don't get it. She used to be as practical as I am.

Her eyes flash. "Those old movies have something we're missing nowadays. Sparks flying, slow burn, passionate love. Just let me have my fantasy."

Fantasy is right. She and Mom have become two peas in a pod. Mom is Hailey Campbell, Clover Park's premier wedding planner and matchmaker extraordinaire (her words). She lives and breathes the fantasy of romance. Me, I'm a realist. Learned that the hard way with a cheating ex and one too many surprise setups from Mom. Oh, the humiliation. The awkwardness. The seething rage.

For a while Mom was low key. Just a few comments here and there. "Rick has a great sense of humor," she'd say. "Very important in a partner." Or, "You can tell a lot by the way a guy treats his sisters. Matthew has four younger sisters who seem to really like him." Or, for one of my many bridesmaid stints, "If you need a wedding date, I've got the perfect guy." All stuff I could nod and smile and move on from. That changed after my first big relationship at twenty-three.

Shawn was my only serious boyfriend. The first guy to make my heart race seeing him across the room. He was affectionate, funny, and smart. Then I discovered Shawn had a longtime girlfriend in his hometown *while he was seeing me*. They're married now. I wish him all the *worst*.

Now I live by the motto *all fun; no expectations*. Why put myself through the heartache?

Mom had other ideas. When I turned twenty-four, she invited a surprise guest to my birthday party who sang me a birthday song. Blaise was a prematurely bald guy in his late twenties wearing a red bowtie and suspenders. With that outfit, I thought he was a singing telegram performer until the song turned into a weird serenade: *Mackenzie's turning twenty-four, even though we've never met before, she's smart, she's beautiful, and soon I hope she'll explore some time with me-e-e-e.*

Uh, no.

When my twenty-fifth birthday rolled around, I was wary, but nothing happened. A week later, while Dad was on a camping trip with the guys, Mom asked me to dress nice for our usual Sunday family dinner. I know, that should've been a red flag, but she's a fashionista with an incredible wardrobe she rarely gets to wear, so I thought she was just trying to level up Sunday dinner. Dad's more a flannel and jeans kind of man.

So I get there, and the table's set all fancy with a white

tablecloth, candles, wine, and three place settings. My brothers are no-shows. It's me, Mom, and Colin, a man I've never met. He looked to be in his thirties and was very smiley. Turned out he was the best man from a recent wedding Mom planned. He confessed immediately he was looking for a good Catholic woman to marry and have children with as soon as possible. Cue me running screaming to the nearest exit.

But I didn't because I. Am. A. Lady. And ladies don't run screaming from their family dinners, even if it turns out your mom has spent the hour before you arrived poring through the family photo albums with a stranger and oversharing about you. I only know this because he confided that he'd also had a terrible haircut before school picture day.

Those pixie-cut pictures were supposed to be burned!

Mom spent most of dinner asking Colin questions and complimenting him on his answers. I felt like I was on a cringe quiz show. What will she win next? A new man!

He wouldn't touch the wine and spoke at length about how unnecessary foul language was. I was starting to wonder if he was an old man trapped in a thirtyish body, but then it all became clear when the moment of truth arrived—dessert.

That was when Colin's parents walked in, greeting me like I was the answer to their prayers. Seemed I was their last hope for grandchildren before Colin took his vow of celibacy to become a priest.

That's right, Mom set me up with a near priest to save his future gene pool.

Colin joined the priesthood. Mom and I had words. I even used some foul language, dammit, which she and Colin both hate.

Mom means well, or so she says. Dad intervened after the priest fiasco and made Mom swear to stop her efforts on my behalf. He told me she made a solemn promise. Even so, I remain vigilant. Valentine's Day could reactivate her match-making instincts.

I turn my attention back to Harper, who's still blocking the door. I think I know why she's having second thoughts about the dance. The guy she loves to hate, Nathan Brooks, is here with a date. Harper would naturally prefer to go in with a date of her own to show him up. It's a weird rivalry thing between them I don't pretend to understand. I work with Nathan, and he's awesome.

I put a hand on her arm. "Nathan's going to be focused on his date, so you don't have to worry about him bugging you. Can we go in now?"

She raises her chin, crossing her arms. "Like I care what he does."

I take advantage of her shift in stance, squeezing between her and the door. Thankfully, she follows me inside. The dance is held in a cool dance studio with a small stage beyond the dance floor, where a jazz band is warming up. They expanded the break room into a large kitchen to accommodate catered events like this. When you live in a small town, people get creative with multi-use buildings.

We head to the coat room and hang up our coats.

"I like being single," I say, a cheery reminder for both of us. "I've dedicated my twenties to casual fun." Thirty is when future me will reconsider my stance.

Harper fluffs her hair, trying to bring out the waves she added with a curling iron. Gravity has already taken its toll. "Yeah, yeah. But when was the last time you actually had casual fun?"

"Shut up."

"You completely gave up on relationships after Shawn."

I walk briskly toward the crowd of family and friends gathered on the dance floor, watching the door for the guests of honor. The jazz band waits while low music plays on the speakers.

"It's not like I haven't seen anyone since him," I throw over my shoulder.

She hurries after me. "Your mom's efforts on your behalf don't count."

I clench my teeth, not liking the reminder. "Remember the lawyer?"

"You lasted one hour. He bored you to tears."

"Yeah, so now I stay away from lawyers. See? I learn."

We join the crowd, exchanging hugs and greetings while we wait. My cousin Mason should've proposed by now; then the plan was to come here to celebrate with everyone. The large dance studio with mirrors along two walls is decorated with streamers and "Congratulations!" balloons. Obviously my family is filled with optimistic romantics. It's a trial I have to bear.

Harper grabs my arm. "Hold on now. I spy tall, dark, and handsome, and he's *not* related." She points her elbow at Mystery Dude.

I look over and suck in air. *Gorgeous. Sexy. Outstanding.* He's built like an athlete—tall, wide shoulders, slim hips. I'm guessing early thirties. He's in a white button-down shirt with gray trousers. His dark brown hair has a slight wave that I'm betting feels like silk. Dark eyes, trimmed beard. *Yes, please!*

His gaze collides with mine. My heart races, and heat rushes from my cheeks down my entire body. I look away from the gorgeous stranger, suddenly realizing he's talking to my matchmaking mom. *Not today, Mom.* A blind date planned by my mother on Valentine's Day is not the way I saw tonight going.

I'm a grown-ass woman who can find my own man.

I am *not* that desperate!

Mason pokes his head in the door, his smile huge. "She said yes!" His new fiancée, May, and her six-year-old daughter, Sophie, walk in, beaming.

"Yeah!" I shout. Everyone cheers with lots of whistles and hooting too. I really like May. She lives across the street from me, owner of the new Serenity Inn.

"You guys!" May exclaims, putting a hand over her heart. Her diamond ring catches the light. "I can't believe you planned all this without me knowing!"

Mason kisses her. They gaze at each other in total adoration as Sophie hugs their legs. For a moment I'm filled with such longing I can barely breathe. What a beautiful moment for this happy little family.

Then I remind myself I like my life just as it is. Light and carefree.

The jazz band starts their music. On my right is a buffet and a drink table catered by Dad's restaurant and bar, Happy Endings. He named it after Mom's romance book club, the Happy Endings Book Club, which is where she got her start as a matchmaker. She takes full credit for every single member finding their happy-ever-after. I'm sure it was just luck and timing. You can't *make* love happen. When someone's ready to get married, they find someone else ready, and then they click because they want the same thing. That's why I look for guys who only want casual fun.

Harper and I go over to congratulate the happy couple. My eye catches on Mom approaching with Mystery Dude. I swear if this is a setup, I'm going to be so pissed.

I force a neutral expression as Mom arrives, smiling her dazzling smile. No sense getting off on a bad foot if she's not matchmaking. Who am I kidding? Of course she is.

Mom's in her fifties now, still strikingly beautiful—long, strawberry-blonde hair, pale blue eyes, flawless skin, and a perfect hourglass figure. Why did I have to take after Dad's side of the family? Ugh. Flat-chested, not much of a curve anywhere. Plain brown hair. At least I'm athletic like Dad. Mom's terrible at most sports. She's afraid of the ball.

Mom gestures toward Mystery Dude. "This is Cal Davis, the new lawyer in town. He used to be a minor league ball player for the triple A Iowa Cubs. Did I get that right?"

"Yes, ma'am." His voice is deeply resonant and warm, like melting chocolate. *I'm so hungry.*

Maybe I don't need to stay away from *all* lawyers.

Mom titters. "Please call me Hailey." She points out each of us by name. When she gets to me, I'm surprised by the depth in his dark brown eyes. Intelligent and searching, like he's trying to see into my soul.

I force myself to lower my gaze, landing on his chest and then lower, oops! Too low. Back to his chest. I'm a furnace in this thin dress. Suddenly the winter air sounds refreshing.

Harper whispers in my ear, "Like what Mom brought you?"

I badly want to elbow her in the kidneys.

"What position did you play?" Mason asks Cal.

"Catcher. Too hard on my knees. They got screwed up."

Mom fills in the rest of his bio. "Then he went to law school, got some experience in the city, and now he's about to take over Gabe Reynolds's practice in town." The city means New York City to locals.

"The city to small-town Clover Park?" I ask. "That's got to be a culture shock."

His gaze locks on mine, and my breath hitches, every nerve ending rising to attention. "I like small towns. I'm from a small town in Minnesota."

Mom wags her finger at Harper and me. "Don't get any ideas about the new single guy in town. He's not the marrying type."

Which is exactly my type!

Cal looks embarrassed and shifts his attention to the room. Probably looking for an out. Clearly, this is not a setup.

Mom pulls me aside to share in a whisper, "His live-in girlfriend broke up with him this morning for not wanting to commit to marriage. It's better to know sooner than later when expectations are mismatched."

I glance back at Cal, who's studying the far wall. I wonder if he heard that.

Mom smiles brightly at him. "Come on, Cal. I'll introduce you to more people."

I take pity on the man. The wound is still fresh for the poor sexy guy.

"I can do it, Mom," I say, attempting to look like I'm not at all interested in him as a gorgeous man who's also conveniently a commitment-phobe.

It's been eight long months.

Mom smiles tightly. "I promised to help him get acclimated to his new hometown. We're good. Right, Cal?"

I keep my voice light. "I'll get him acquainted with the under-forty crowd since he's clearly under forty."

Her eyes narrow. She firmly believes age is just a number, as she'll tell anyone who mentions getting older. Cal looks from me to Mom, seeming unsure what to do.

The music changes to a slow song, Etta James's "At Last."

Mom sighs dramatically. "Okay, Mackenzie, but whatever you do, don't slow dance with him. The last thing I need is my daughter getting drawn in by another player. No offense, Cal."

Yup, she said that. Mom has no filter when it comes to protecting her kids. She believes I'm frequently taken in by "players" because she'll often hear from the small-town grapevine that I was seen out with a guy, and when she follows up with me, I crush her romantic hopes by telling her we're not seeing each other anymore. She never believes it's me who keeps it casual. It's her love goggles that keep her from seeing clearly.

"More of a baseball player," Cal mumbles. Of course no one wants to be labeled a player, but any guy who just got out of a live-in relationship for commitment issues isn't going to want more of the same. He's perfect.

I tilt my head toward the dance floor. He follows me without a word.

A few moments later, I wrap my arms around his neck, leaving just enough space between us for decency. He radiates heat and pheromones. Mmm, he smells so good. A clean, crisp scent. Cologne? Him? I don't know, and I don't care. Cal is the perfect man to end this damn dry spell.

On the other hand, he did just go through a major breakup.

Is he even into me?

I'll know by the end of the party.

Cal

I've already met a lot of people in town thanks to Hailey, which is crucial for building a client list, and now I'm dancing with her sexy daughter. I noticed Mackenzie right away. When her eyes met mine, a jolt of lust hit me by surprise, especially after the day I've had.

She's about a foot shorter than me, even in her spiked heels. Her dress clings to her athletic body, ending mid-thigh. I gulp. It's just a dance. One dance to be polite.

If you had told me I'd go from dodging law books to dancing with a sexy stranger today, I'd have thought you were nuts. That's right. Law books. Thrown at my head.

In answer to Rayna's demand for marriage, I said in my most reasonable tone, "What's the rush?"

Boy, was that the wrong thing to say. She blew up, saying we were both in our thirties and that's what normal people do. Then she threw my briefcase and law books at me. All this happened before noon. She woke up expecting big things, and it went downhill from there. I'm more relieved than sad, which I guess says a lot about our relationship.

Before she moved into my apartment, Rayna was cool and casual. Things were easy between us. Then my roommate moved out, Rayna's lease ran out on her place, and she asked if she could move in with me while she looked for a new place. Rent in the city isn't cheap, and rentals go fast. Even so, I looked for another male roommate and asked her to use her extensive network to find her own place. Nothing panned out, so I offered my place as a *temporary* solution.

I was very firm—six months max for her to find a new apartment, giving me time to find a new roommate. She agreed. Honestly, I liked her a lot. I just wasn't in deep-emotion territory. I never am. Not since...anyway, after she moved in, Rayna went into overdrive on the couple thing.

Candlelit dinners, little gifts and love notes left around the apartment, a new social schedule with her married couple friends, even a vacation that was couples only. It got so I couldn't relax at home and spent most of my time at the office.

She veered between the silent treatment and yelling. I knew I was disappointing her, but I could barely breathe in our shared space. She wasn't having any luck finding a new place, and I quietly decided to let her take over my lease when it ran out, and move somewhere else. I was just waiting for the right time to tell her. I had hoped we could keep seeing each other, even if we didn't live together. It was only supposed to be a temporary arrangement, after all.

But then she started spending a lot of time with her ex. She told me it was platonic, he was her best friend again, and I was too closed off to meet her emotional needs.

I wasn't happy about all the time they spent together, but I also knew he had a girlfriend. When he got engaged, Rayna was upset. That's why she suddenly wanted us to get married. Not because of me, because of him. I guess Valentine's Day upped the stakes.

"Welcome to Clover Park," Mackenzie says near my ear, rocketing me back to the present.

"Thank you," I say politely, shifting back a little. There's this incredible heat radiating off her body. Or is that heat between our bodies? She's so sexy, and I can't even believe I notice that with today's breakup. That's compartmentalizing for you.

Her blue eyes meet mine, and my mouth goes dry. "Long shot, but do you know Sutton Davis? She's from Minnesota, too, and, you know, same last name."

A corner of my mouth lifts. "Sure, I know everyone in the great state of Minnesota."

"Smartass."

I grin. "Sutton's my little sister. That's how I heard about Clover Park and Gabe Reynolds looking for someone to take over his law practice. She subscribes to the *Clover Park*

Record." My sister is a ball of sunshine, always bright and enthusiastic. She's a full-time virtual assistant for Brooks Campbell Security here in Clover Park.

"She works for me!"

It suddenly clicks. Mackenzie's mom is Hailey Campbell. "You're the extraordinary Mackenzie Campbell?"

She laughs. "Yes! And she's extraordinary too. Her research skills are amazing. She can take technical specs from any industry and translate that into a report that's the basis of every proposal we put together. And she's fast!"

"She goes on and on about you. Mackenzie's so smart. Mackenzie runs the place with confident authority. Mackenzie can do anything."

She tosses her hair. "It's nice to have a fan."

I can't seem to look away from her sparkling blue eyes. This is a woman who likes to have fun, and when was the last time I had fun? Rayna was an activist, always angry and worked up over one cause or another. Then there was my job. Corporate law isn't exactly a joyride. Only my pro bono work for the women's shelter brought satisfaction.

"Any chance you could get her to move here?" she asks. "I've asked her more than once, but she always dodges the question. Maybe with her brother in town…"

"I wish she would. She's been with her crap boyfriend since high school, and he's not going anywhere."

She stills, shifting back to look up at me. "Why is her boyfriend crap?"

"He doesn't appreciate her like he should. Sutton's special."

She gives me a soft smile. "That's so sweet. What a nice brother you are." She shifts closer. An inconvenient spike of raw lust hits.

"Just the truth."

Would it be so bad to have a little fun?

Yes.

I don't do casual hookups. I've had a series of relationships that all ended…badly. Hmm, maybe time to change things up?

What am I even thinking? I know better than to jump into a relationship right after a breakup. Besides, it's a bad professional move. I just got here. Trust and a good reputation are everything in a small town like Clover Park. Those were Gabe Reynolds's exact words when he hired me. I owe it to him to keep the stellar reputation of his law practice intact.

The music must've changed to another slow song at some point. I didn't notice. I spy her parents, Josh and Hailey, dancing. They talk as they dance close, a natural rhythm between them. Reminds me of my parents when I was a kid. They used to roll the living room rug back to dance and really let loose. I didn't know how rare their happiness was as a kid. I just thought they were embarrassing. No wonder Dad never got over her.

"What else did Sutton say about me?" Mackenzie asks with a cheeky grin.

"She says if she lived closer, she'd like to hang with you." I grimace. "I'm not sure if I was supposed to share that."

Her hand goes to her chest. "No, it's nice! I always thought the same thing. Funny she never mentioned you."

"Obviously she idolizes me."

"Ha! I'd love to take her on in a larger role if she lived closer."

I lift my brows. "Okay if I tell her that?"

"I'll do it. Do you think she'll marry that guy?"

"Not anytime soon. He's still sowing his wild oats."

She steps back, looking outraged. "Does she know he's cheating on her?"

"She knows, but doesn't want to know. He always explains away suspicious activity. I've tried to talk to her about it, but she gets defensive."

"Hmm…"

"Yeah."

She draws close again. I hold her stiffly at the waist, preventing any further closeness. Just feels safer that way.

She gives me a sweet smile. "I like dancing with you."

I clear my throat. *Just be polite.* "Yeah, me too."

We're quiet for the rest of the dance, but somehow that makes it worse. Her hand slides from my shoulder to my elbow in a warm path, easing my stiff hold on her waist until she's moved so close our bodies brush against each other as we sway, a little brush to my chest; her chin brushes my shoulder. It would be rude to push her away.

The heat builds between us, a sparking tension, like our bodies are communicating on a primal level. This is bad. As soon as this song ends, I'm outta here.

The song ends, and she grabs my hand. "Come on, I'll introduce you to everyone."

I follow her.

2

Mackenzie

After dragging Cal around the room to meet everyone, where he was amazingly chill and friendly, I decide to be brave and drop a hint to see if he's interested in casual fun. Sure, there was chemistry on the dance floor, but he did just get dumped earlier today. It's a little strange how unfazed he seems after a major breakup. I mean, they lived together. If I broke up with someone I lived with, I'd be devastated.

On the other hand, he's not giving me monk vibes. Maybe casual fun is the stress relief we both need.

Mom and Dad approach me near the end of the dance, already wearing their coats. "Dad and I have plans," Mom chirps.

I nod with a bland expression. *No details, please.* It's late on Valentine's Day, and let's just say they're still hot for each other.

Dad wraps an arm around Mom's shoulders. He's got a little gray in his dark brown hair, but otherwise in top shape. He's a former soldier with a mischievous streak that's legend, especially concerning the escalating prank war he and Mom got into before they were married. People in town still talk about it.

"Can you and Harper take the catering dishes back to

Happy Endings?" Dad asks. "They're all washed and ready to go."

I smile. "Absolutely. No worries."

I hug them goodbye. They walk out holding hands, stealing glances at each other like they can't wait to be alone. This is why I'm in no rush to settle down. They set the bar high. I didn't even attempt a relationship until I was twenty-three, and Shawn was a huge disappointment. Now I understand that what my parents have is rare. It's only logical to stick to casual when that kind of relationship doesn't come around often.

I look around for Cal. He's talking to my younger brother, Cooper, and his fiancée, Rowan. Cooper can talk to anyone. He's a bartender at Happy Endings and soon to be co-owner. I know why my parents asked me and Harper to deal with the catering dishes instead of Cooper. We're the only two without plans on this most romantic of nights. Though that could be changing.

I head over to Cal, Cooper, and Rowan just as Harper walks over barefoot, holding her heels by the straps. "Hey, all." She turns to me. "I'm beat. Let's go."

"Dad asked if we could drop off the catering dishes at Happy Endings."

She groans. "Because we're the only single people here. It's like a double tax. Single on Valentine's *and* working overtime."

Cal lifts a hand. "I can help if you want to go home, Harper."

That was easy. Maybe he wants time alone with me too.

Harper gives me a sideways questioning glance, which I answer with a telepathic *hell yes!*

"That would be great," I say brightly.

Harper turns to Cooper. "Can I get a ride home with you and Rowan?"

He waves pretend fumes away from his face. "Only if you put your shoes back on."

She waggles them in his face in retaliation. Cooper and

Rowan jump back. "They're not that bad!" She puts her heels on, wincing, and waves at me. "Bye, enjoy your Valentine's after dark."

My stomach flutters with excitement, but I manage to sound casual. "Bye, guys."

The three of them head out.

I look at Cal. "Where's your car?"

"I parked at Ludbury House. Your mom wanted to meet me there so she'd have time to get to know me on the ride over here."

"Sounds about right. Ludbury House is only a block from my house, so that makes it easy. I can drop you off by your car after Happy Endings. Let me grab a cart."

We head to the back room, my mind already skipping three steps ahead—Happy Endings, alone in an area only employees have access to; no, we'll go to his hotel. Much more room to maneuver in a bed; then I'll drop him off in the lot. I'm going for it. It's now or never.

"Your feet must be killing you in those heels," he says. Funny, most guys wouldn't even think about my comfort level. Well, he does have a sister. He must be well versed in women's fashion complaints.

"Nope. I've been practicing walking in heels since I was a preschooler. Mom has an extensive shoe collection. Besides, these were my Valentine's gift."

"Ah." He glances at me. "From whom?"

"Me."

He grins. "I didn't know that was a thing. Women getting themselves gifts on Valentine's Day."

"I know best what I like, so why not?"

I grab a two-shelf cart and wheel it out to the table with the large covered stainless steel dishes. Cal takes a dish by the handles and puts it on the lower shelf of the cart. He bends slowly like he's being careful of his knees. I bet giving up baseball was hard for him.

We work in tandem, accomplishing the task quickly.

"Are these going to fit in your car?" he asks as he pushes the cart toward the exit.

"You ask me that *now*?" I tease.

"Right."

"The trunk is roomy, and the back seats fold down. No problem. I've done it before many times."

The lot's empty except for my Honda Accord. I chose this car for its reliability because I'd rather spend money on cute shoes than a pricey car. Also, I can't afford a pricey car. Ha-ha.

We load up the car and get inside. I glance over at him in the passenger seat. His knees come up high because there's not enough leg room. "You can push the seat back farther with the handle on the side." I start the car and back out of the space.

He adjusts it, looking only a little less squished.

I shift gears and head out. "Guess they didn't make this car with a tall person in mind."

"I'm not even that tall. Six four."

"Tall to me. If you were seven feet or eight, you'd need to ride around in a van."

"A van? Try a custom car. That's what the pro basketball players do."

"Ever consider basketball?"

"I played it in high school, but baseball was always my favorite."

When I pull up to a red light, I turn to him and get right to the point. "How do you feel about casual fun with me tonight?"

He clears his throat. "I feel favorably."

I grin. "Excellent. After we drop off the dishes."

He's quiet. I hope that means he's imagining all the dirty things we can do to each other. I sure am.

~

Cal

I'm having trouble wrapping my head around the fact that

this morning I was living with Rayna, then I went to a Valentine's Day dance (first time for that), and now I'm with an incredibly sexy woman who radiates warmth and kindness. Something sorely missing in my life.

When she introduced me to her family and friends, it was clear how much she loves them. She remembered everyone's latest news, gave out compliments like candy, and sang my praises as the new Clover Park lawyer, even though she knows next to nothing about me. I guess being Sutton's older brother gives me some credibility.

She left out the one fact that most people find interesting about me, that I was a ball player. Maybe she doesn't find it interesting. It was a relief not to have to share over and over how my knees got screwed up and I had to quit. I'll probably have to get knee replacements at some point, but I'm putting it off as long as I can. Not my favorite topic.

In short, she's irresistible, and I want to give her whatever keeps that bright smile on her face.

I follow her in the back door of Happy Endings, carrying a stack of catering dishes, through a kitchen with three workers, and into a large supply closet. She turns on the light and sets her dishes on a back shelf. I put mine next to hers.

She turns, locks the door behind us, and whispers, "Kiss me."

I pull at the collar of my button-down shirt. "Here? We're doing this here? There's workers, and isn't this your family's restaurant?"

She wraps her arms around my neck and presses her body against mine. I'm rock hard in an instant. "It's just a kiss." She goes on tiptoe but can't quite reach me.

I lean down and give her a soft kiss. She opens for me, her tongue teasing, sending lightning down my spine. The kiss turns carnal. She tries to climb my body, her leg wrapping around mine, seeking contact with urgently aching parts. I pick her up by the waist, and she wraps her legs around me. Raw need consumes me. I don't care that there's people right outside. I press her back against the door, lost in sensation. Oh God, she tastes so good, like mint and sex. I need more.

She pulls back to look at me, running her finger along my jaw. "You passed the kiss test."

My mind tosses that strange comment aside in favor of another kiss. She puts her hand on my chest and pushes. I lift my head. "Yeah?"

She lowers her legs and slides down my fully aroused body. I stifle a groan. She takes my hand. "Cal, I want to be crystal clear. This is a one-night event. Just casual fun. Agree?"

I stare at her luscious lips, so soft. *More, more, more.*

"Okay, Cal? Nothing serious."

I snap to attention. "I just ended a live-in relationship. It's not like I'm going to propose after meeting you."

"That's perfect because I don't believe in love. At least not for this stage in my life."

"Sure," I murmur, stroking her hair back from her face, leaning down to kiss along the column of her throat. She tips her head back with a sigh.

There's a knock at the door. I jerk back.

A male voice calls, "Mackenzie, we're closing soon."

"Be out in a sec." She takes a deep breath, then opens the door. The workers are cleaning up the kitchen. "Bye, everyone!"

"Hi, how ya doing?" I say to the guys, careful to keep Mackenzie in front of me to hide the obvious.

"I didn't know you had company in there," a middle-aged man in a chef's hat says.

"No one needs to know, Pete," she returns.

He puts his hands up. "I won't tell."

She pulls me at a near run to the back door, laughing, and out to the lot where she parked. Pure exhilaration fires through me. There's something fun about sneaking out and heading to our next clandestine location. She unlocks the car remotely and gets in the driver's side while I slide in the passenger side.

We're not even out of the lot when she asks, "Do your knees hurt doing different, uh, activities?"

Is she asking about sex positions?

I have a feeling what you see is what you get with Mackenzie. I like that straightforward honesty, even if it's awkward to dive into sex talk before we get to bed.

Before I can answer, she peels out of the lot so fast my head hits the headrest. She says, "I've got a roommate. Where're you staying?"

"I'm about twenty minutes from here in the Ethan Allen hotel."

"Got it. So, back to those knees, do they bother you on rainy days or in certain positions?" She lets out a small laugh. "You lifted me, and I'm no lightweight. Just trying to make sure no one gets hurt."

"You're light to me."

She scoffs. "Okay. How bad are your knees? Tonight's all about pleasure."

I shift uncomfortably, my boner not going anywhere. I realize too late that she's already speeding out of town, and I probably should've met her at the hotel in my car. "Basically, as long as I'm not doing squats or a lot of kneeling, I get by fine. The rest of me is still in athlete form."

She glances over at me. "I noticed."

"I noticed you too."

"My athletic form?"

"Your sexy form."

"God, I want you."

My gut tightens as desire blazes through me. "Mutual," I croak.

She squeezes my arm. "I've got condoms in my purse, so no worries."

Heat creeps up my neck. I've never spoken so openly with a woman before we get naked. "Great."

She smiles, glances at me, and does a double take. "Are you blushing?"

"It's the streetlights casting weird shadows."

"This is going to be so fun."

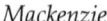

Mackenzie

The moment we get to Cal's hotel room, we collide in a passionate kiss. All my doing because I throw myself at him. I missed this passion in my life. I unbutton his shirt and pull it off him. Then I shimmy off my dress, standing in my red lace panties and bra. He gets naked at lightning speed, his eyes eating me up as I slip off my bra and panties.

I pull back the covers and bounce into bed. He joins me, rolling me to my side so we're chest to chest. His big hand cradles my jaw as he kisses me again, only this time he's more tender. No, tender is for lovers. This is just sex. I bite his lower lip. He jolts, but then he's all in. Urgent and raw, the kiss turns wild, his hands roaming all over me.

Yes, yes, yes. The bold assurance in his hands tells me he knows what he's doing. I'm ready for him. Now.

I push him onto his back and climb on top of him. His dark eyes look glazed, almost like shock and awe, like this experience is new for him. But that can't be. Don't gorgeous ball players get their pick of women?

He brushes my hair back from my face, his voice husky. "I've never done anything like this before. Meet and go to bed."

"Me either," I lie. I guess the commitment-phobe waits for the second or third date, but I say why postpone pleasure? I'm choosy with men, but I know when someone's a good pick for me.

I kiss him, reveling in his sensual lips, his clean scent, and the powerful body beneath mine. I reach for my purse to retrieve the condom when he stops me.

"Whoa, slow down. If I only get one night, I want to make it last."

"Oh, right. Let me get prepared."

He waits for me to set a condom on the nightstand, and

then rolls me to my back. His arms rest on either side of me, holding his weight. He brushes the lightest of kisses on the corners of my lips and then another light kiss in the center.

He kisses me like he has all night. I'm restless beneath him, used to a fast ride, but within moments I'm melting into the mattress. His fingers slide along my neck, bringing a shiver.

Sweet, slow, and easy. That's Cal's deal. And I feel too good to move things along.

He lifts his head, his deep voice rough, scraping against my insides. "I can't get enough of you."

My lips part. I'm momentarily dazed. He kisses my chin, my cheeks, the sensitive spot below my ear. And then it's nothing but soft sighs as he learns my body, coaxing pleasure from every part of me from my head to my toes, lingering in my favorite spots long enough to draw out moans and total abandon. My climax hits hard, cascading sensation after sensation that leaves me spent.

When he finally joins with me, our gazes lock, and a shock of emotions washes over me. I close my eyes. I don't know him well enough to feel so much. Like a meeting of souls. It's only because he went too slow.

Disturbed, I urge him on, rocking under him, kissing him passionately, putting my all into losing myself in the physical. He cradles my jaw, kissing me urgently as he rocks into me. *Yes, right there.* I come apart, white-hot pleasure consuming me. He goes over a few moments later, his breath harsh in my ear.

I stare at the curve of his shoulder blindly. Holy shit. Best sex of my life hands down. His weight on me feels crazy good. I kinda want to hug him and thank him for his spectacular everything.

He nuzzles into my neck, and I sigh. *No, no sighing.* This after-hookup cuddling is completely against the rules. I know it; he knows it. I've got to get out of here before I get sucked in. And what was that gazing stuff about? That was *not* what we agreed to. Someone has to make the boundaries clear.

I push at his chest. He takes the hint, rolling to my side and pulling me in close. Skin to skin, the body heat between us is incredible. My eyes droop. I'm so warm and satisfied and safe.

My eyes open in alarm. Safe? I just met the guy. What is wrong with me? I hurry out of bed and start getting dressed.

He props up on an elbow. "Where're you going? Spend the night."

"Can't. I have an early morning appointment." *With my comfy bed.* "Get dressed. I'll drive you to your car."

"Too tired."

I wiggle my dress down over my hips and turn on the overhead light. He squints against the harsh light. "I have to drive you back to Ludbury House to get your car. Mom will notice it. That's her place of business. She may have a wedding tomorrow."

"I'll get a ride there first thing tomorrow. Night."

And in the bright light of the hotel room, this man with tousled brown hair and the physique of an athlete promptly falls asleep.

I need to go. Casual only works with clear boundaries. There's absolutely no reason to stay.

He's so beautiful.

I pull the covers up over him, tempted to smooth his hair, but I resist. I turn off the light and leave quickly and quietly, stopping in the hallway for a few deep calming breaths.

Some mysterious force has me turning around to stare at his hotel door, imagining him opening it and welcoming me back into his arms. I suck in air. This is so not like me.

That's not how this works.

I square my shoulders and walk over to punch the button for the elevator, ignoring the pang of regret. I know the rules.

I step into the elevator and push the "close door" button rapidly until it finally closes. I let out a breath. Cal and I are finished, forever and ever. Unless, God forbid, I find myself in need of a lawyer.

I'm sitting in the kitchen, innocently eating my usual humongous salad lunch, when my mind flashes to Cal on top of me, his deep gaze, the rush of unwanted feelings. I shake my head, coming back to the present to find my cat, Felix, staring at me from across the room.

"I don't have any tuna," I inform Felix. "Later. After grocery shopping."

He's a tuxedo cat, gray with a white mustache and white chest. It used to be that Felix only loved me, but when Cooper's fiancée, Rowan, lived with me and Harper briefly, Felix devoted himself to her too. In all fairness, she was a jilted bride at the time, and my boy here senses heartbreak. Not that I'm heartbroken. I had a fun, strangely intimate one-night stand. No problem.

I avoid Felix's stare, banishing thoughts of Cal from my mind. The memory of last night flooded back the moment I woke up, then again on my run, in the shower. I spear a cucumber slice. Maybe I should go for another run to clear my head.

Felix rubs against my leg with a shaky tail. He's excited to be near me and ever hopeful for tuna. I stroke his cheek and give him a scratch on top of his head.

"Hel-lo," Harper carols as she walks into the kitchen, holding a cheerful bouquet of flowers and a shopping bag. We live in a house paid for by our close friend, Shayla Adler. She's a movie star like Harper's mom. I know, we're so lucky. Shayla briefly lived here, too, with her assistant, but then she got together with her long-lost love, Harper's older brother, Owen. At least I don't have to worry about me or Harper leaving for a guy. Neither one of us wants man complications at this point in our lives.

"Someone's got an admirer," she says, giving me a sly look. "Found these on the porch. So-o-o, how was it last night?"

My heart hammers. "Those are for me?" I thought the flowers were one of her impulse buys. She's the kind of person to go to the store for one thing and come home with three more. I go with a list. What can I say, I was an accounting major. I like rules, order, and exact numbers. I'm also an excellent saver.

She plucks the card out of the bouquet and tries to hand it to me, but I evade it neatly. "Card has your name on it."

We had one simple rule, Cal! Casual. It has to be from him, or Harper wouldn't be enjoying this so much. I like rules, dammit!

I cross my arms. "You keep it. No, toss it."

She grabs my hand and pushes the small envelope into it. "Don't be weird. It's for you. So how was it with the ball player? It was good, right? You're glowing."

"I am not glowing. I just got a lot of sleep and went for a run this morning."

"You always go for a run and come back looking haggard."

"Thanks a lot."

"It's beyond me why you torture yourself with running."

I can't seem to take my eyes off the flowers. They're not bargain after-Valentine's Day roses. It's a pretty arrangement of pink tulips, white carnations, baby's breath, and mini daisies. I lift my hair from the nape of my neck. It's unbearably hot in here.

I tuck the note back in the flowers she's holding. "You keep them. Put them in your room, okay?"

"What's the matter?"

"Nothing. I just don't like carnations."

"Mac."

"Mac is a truck. It's Mackenzie."

"You *are* a truck." She opens the small envelope and pulls out the card, smiling. "Sweet." I bet she read it earlier on the porch. She tucks the card back into the envelope. "Wanna know what it says?" Her eyes sparkle mischievously. Like this is a fun game. It's not. *Someone* crossed the line after we explicitly set the rules for a no-hard-feelings encounter.

"They're from Cal," she says like I don't know.

Felix stands on my leg, and I scoop him up, rubbing my chin on top of his soft head.

Harper sighs and sets the bouquet on the counter. "At least put them in a vase. These are better than the kind you get at the supermarket."

"Fine, but they're going in your room."

She shrugs and starts emptying her bag onto the counter —half-price Valentine's chocolate truffles, a hairbrush, chip clips, and lip gloss. She originally went for the candy.

I go back to eating lunch, my hands a little shaky. Why would Cal send me flowers? We agreed last night was the end and for good reason. He's coming out of a relationship, and he's a commitment-phobe. The last thing I want is the heartache of an unsatisfying relationship, and that's what it would be with him. Classic rebound situation.

And I hate to even let this influence my thinking, but Mom told me to stay away from him, and she's *never* wrong about people. It's what makes her so good at networking and building a client list.

What could Cal have possibly written in that note that made Harper say *sweet*?

I hoped with him staying in a hotel out of town and his law office situated on a side street I can easily avoid, that I wouldn't have any reminders of him. Well, at least for long enough to stop thinking about him. When the memory isn't so fresh.

How did he know where I live? He must've looked me up. This is so wrong. It's worse than wrong. Actually, I'm pissed. Pissed with a capital *P*. I was enjoying a peaceful lunch with my demanding cat staring at me and now this.

I push back from the table, march over to the offending bouquet, and throw it in the trash.

Harper gives me side-eye. "Is this because your mom told you to stay away from him and you didn't and now you feel guilty?"

I snort. "This has nothing to do with Mom. Cal and I agreed it was a onetime thing for many legit reasons."

"Because you're afraid of love."

"I'm not afraid." I glare at her. "I seem to remember Nathan sent you flowers out of the blue last Halloween—"

"Who sends Halloween flowers?"

"And *you* freaked out. Nathan was trying to mend fences, even though he has no idea what he did to make you hate him." Nathan is my business partner, a loyal, solid guy. He was Harper's neighbor growing up, and they used to be close.

"Oh, he knows what he did," Harper says grimly.

"What did he do?"

She pulls the bouquet out of the trash can under the kitchen sink. "Good thing you just emptied the trash. That would've been gross." She gets a vase from the cabinet and starts filling it with water.

I clench my jaw. "Don't you see Cal's breaking the rules of engagement? I never would've hooked up with him if I'd known he'd completely ignore the boundaries we set out in the beginning. There are rules for a reason."

"Uh-huh."

She plucks the card from the bouquet and puts it on my

head. I let it fall to the floor. Felix bats it, and it hits the baseboard by the sink. I stare at the mystery card, torn between throwing it away and reading it.

Dammit, lawyers like Cal are supposed to follow the rules, color inside the lines. I went on a date with a lawyer once, and he may have bored me to tears, but he was definitely a rule follower.

I huff. "Cal must be a terrible lawyer. I bet he defended criminals."

"Someone has to." She sets the flowers in the vase and arranges them a bit. They are lovely. "Also, don't you remember he said he did corporate law, or were you too busy admiring his tall, dark, and handsome self?"

"It was fun. End of story."

She snatches the notecard off the floor. "Methinks you doth protest too much."

"I don't!" *His dark soulful eyes as we joined.*

"Mmm-hmm." She removes the note from the envelope, sticks it under a magnet on the fridge, and puts away the chip clips. I stare at her, refusing to read the note. She uses the lip gloss, tucks it in her purse, and then opens the bag of chocolate truffles, unwrapping one and putting it in her mouth. "Want one?" she asks around the candy.

"Not until I finish lunch. Thank you."

"Is that a rule your mom taught you? This is our house. No rules, baby."

I snatch a truffle from the bag.

She snorts. "So easy. Oh! Felix is licking your salad. Did you have some tuna in there?"

"Felix! No! It was leftover pork chop."

"Looks like you need a fresh salad from the fridge." She sounds smug. She leaves, twirling her hairbrush.

I scoop Felix off the table. "You don't deserve tuna." I set him on the floor, and he delicately washes his face with a paw, looking pleased with himself.

I dump the salad into the trash, my eyes catching on the

bouquet in its full glory in a glass vase on the counter. Ugh, Harper was supposed to take this with her.

I pull out a fresh plate and turn to the fridge. See, this is exactly why Harper put the note here. She knew hunger would win out over moral principles. I steel myself against any sweet sentiment.

Hope we can meet up again.
   Cal

I swallow hard. Maybe he meant he's hoping for another hookup. My stomach dips, an ache of reminder of the incredible pleasure. Slow hands, endless kisses, the heat. My God, the heat.

Would it be so bad to have one more night?

I snatch the card from the fridge and drop it in the trash.

Brooks Campbell Security has a regular Monday afternoon meeting in our office in town. Our company is three equal partners—Nathan Brooks, Owen Campbell (my cousin), and me. Nathan's name comes first because he contributed the most money to founding the company. I do the accounting, marketing, and logistics to keep everything running smoothly. Nathan and Owen work on location with our clients for high-tech security systems and cybersecurity.

Business is doing much better than this time last year. We added clients from the entertainment industry, thanks to Owen's connections through his wife, Shayla, and Nathan's close to a deal with the finance sector in the city. This is in addition to work we've already established in pharma and tech companies.

I bundle up in my hat and black down coat for the short walk to our office on Main Street. We're in a converted apartment above Something's Brewing Café. I left enough time to get a latte. It's nice to get out of the house and focus on work.

I take one step onto our porch, spy Cal Davis across the street, shoveling snow for some reason, and do an about-face, practically leaping back inside. I shut the door and lean against it, my heart in my throat. *Okay, deep breath.*

Let's look at this logically. Cal's shoveling snow from the front sidewalk of the Serenity Inn. He's either a really bad lawyer needing a side gig, or he's helping out while living at the inn right across the street from me. Why couldn't he stay at that nice out-of-town hotel?

I freely admit our hookup was a mistake and completely initiated by me. Lesson learned. Don't jump into bed with a guy with soulful eyes. It'll twist you around until you don't know what's fun and what's real.

Harper walks into our front room with her laptop and settles on the cushy red velvet sofa. She mostly works at home as a graphic designer. "Why are you leaning against the door? Don't you have a meeting?"

I set my satchel down and peek out the front window. Yup. Still there. "Cal's shoveling snow at the inn. Right out front."

She joins me at the window. "He's probably just helping out. Mason shoveled this morning, but we got more snow since he left for work."

"Okay, new plan. I'll drive to work."

Her brows lift. "Seriously?"

I'm being ridiculous. My office is half a block away on Main Street. I don't care. I need a safe perimeter away from Cal.

She gives me an exasperated look. "You're going to have to deal with him at some point now that he works in town. I heard his apartment won't be ready until March first." News travels fast in a small town.

"Right, okay. It's not like he's staying across the street for me. Maybe he wanted to get started at work right away in light of his breakup, and this has nothing to do with me. He probably wants to organize his new office. Right? That's what I would do."

Harper gives me side-eye. "Right." She goes back to her laptop.

"And May must be happy to have a paying guest. It's tough when you're starting a new business." May's a single mom brave enough to start the inn to follow her dream. Well, she was a single mom. Soon to be married to Mason.

"Exactly. I'm sure Cal's forgotten all about you. Mackenzie who?"

I glare at her, but she's too busy on her laptop to notice. It's only been three days since Cal and I, err, connected. I turn back to the front window to keep an eye on May's first paying guest. "Of course I'm happy for May."

As if Cal senses my staring, he turns, catches my eye, and waves. Mortified at being caught staring, I lift a palm and step back from the window.

My heart races. I can't leave the house now. It looks like I was spying on him.

I turn to Harper, distraught. "He waved."

She gasps in mock horror. "How intimate."

I worry my lower lip. Am I going to have to pretend I didn't see this man in his naked glory every time I leave the house?

I yank my hat off and turn to Harper. She looks so serene as she works it makes me more agitated. "The out-of-town hotel was nice, too. I don't know why he wanted to move hotels."

"I bet May's giving him a good long-term rate. Of course, if he wants the lowest rate, we could use a roommate." She grins. "We could make him shovel snow, take out the trash, and kill bugs for us."

My back gets up. "We don't need a man around for those crappy chores. I can do crappy chores as well as any man."

"Great. They're all yours."

I shut my mouth with a snap. I walked into that one.

I check the time. I'm starting to sweat in my winter coat. I need to go.

I shift casually over to the sofa, being careful not to be seen through the front window. "Is he still there?"

She doesn't look up. "You said it meant nothing."

"Not nothing. I just planned on moving on."

"Then say hi to our new neighbor and go to work. He'll see you're moving on just fine."

I jam my hat back on. "Maybe I will."

"Good. 'Cause I sure don't want to listen to you bitch about your casual fling for the next two weeks. The man has to live somewhere."

Cal

After shoveling the front walk, I put some rock salt down to keep the ice away. Being from Minnesota, dealing with snow and ice is second nature for me. I'm finishing up when my eye catches on Mackenzie marching straight for me. She doesn't look happy. Were the flowers too much? I just wanted to give her a gift like she gave me by turning my day around. And if she's open to it, I wouldn't mind another night like that.

I meet her halfway. "Hi."

"Hi," she says tensely, looking anywhere but at me. "I live right there." She stabs a finger in the direction of her house.

"I know. I looked you up for the flowers. Did you like them?"

She waves that away and finally meets my eyes with a hard look. Damn if I'm not drawn in again. Angry, happy, in the throes of pleasure, doesn't matter. She's the most beautiful woman I've ever met. Her light gray knit hat frames her face —the color is high in her cheeks, her sky blue eyes bright, her lips pink. Her long dark hair is just as soft as it looks.

"Stop looking at me like that," she snaps.

"Like what?"

"Like, you know."

I feign innocence. "I don't know."

She presses her lips in a flat line. "Cal, let me be very clear. No more contact between us beyond a friendly wave from a distance. Call it the law of the one-night stand."

I suppress a laugh. "The law of the one-night stand, huh? I must've missed that class in law school."

She crosses her arms. "Obviously."

I shift closer, lowering my voice. "I had a good time that night. I—"

"Do you remember what we talked about before our hotel time? Because I sure do. I'm not looking for anything serious in this phase of my life, and you just got out of a live-in relationship for not being able to commit, which is *fine*. Great, actually. That's why I moved forward with you, but I'm getting the distinct feeling—"

"Hey, relax. It was fun."

She pulls fuzzy white gloves from her pockets, and one falls on the ground. I pick it up and offer it to her. She ignores me, pulling on the other one. "Exactly. It was fun. Past tense. Glad we understand each other."

I take her hand and carefully slide the glove on. She stares at my hand. Once the glove's on, I hold her smaller hand in mine and dip my head to catch her eye. "If we both agree this isn't serious, what's the harm of a repeat?"

She slides her hand from mine and looks at me suspiciously. "Like a friends-with-benefits situation?"

I lean down, my lips a breath away from hers. "Without the friends part."

Her breath hitches in anticipation. I can't disappoint her. I kiss her, tender and then deeper. She kisses me back with complete abandon, her arms wrapping around my neck. That kind of lusty abandon is rare. I fucking love it.

She pulls away abruptly, seeming embarrassed. "I have a work meeting."

"Stop by tonight."

"Maybe." She shakes her head. "I don't know."

I snag her by the waist of her coat, drawing her close for one last, lingering kiss. "Think about it."

Her expression is wary with a hint of longing and, underneath all that, vulnerable. Does she know how her emotions show on her face? She'd be terrible at poker. I watch as she walks away, the cute pompon on her hat bouncing in time to her rapid steps.

I hope longing wins out because I can't forget the night we had together. Maybe I'll suggest strip poker. Ha.

4
_____

Mackenzie

We meet up at midnight. I tiptoe into his room, careful not to alert anyone I know at the inn to my presence. Let's just say—

Yes.

And yes!

And yes, yes, yes!

The man is bossy in the bedroom. The faster I surrender, the greater the reward. So hot.

Every night is better than the one before.

No one has to know.

5

Coffee time. I whistle as I walk down Catoonah Street toward Main Street. I've been pulling some late nights with Mackenzie. Not complaining. With Gabe, the retiring lawyer, away on a third honeymoon (I had no idea that was a thing), work doesn't start for another week. Mackenzie comes over every night on her own initiative, texting me to ask if the coast is clear. She's a wonder—open, enthusiastic, sensual. Clover Park has been *very* welcoming to me so far.

For a small town, it's really got everything. All roads lead to Main Street. My favorite spots so far are the bookstore, Something's Brewing Café with the best coffee on earth, the ice-cream shop, the pizza place, and Happy Endings, a bar and restaurant. Away from the main business district, there's a few churches and Ludbury House, the historic mansion where Hailey works as a wedding planner. Nice lady. She texted me this morning to see if I needed anything.

I told her that her sexy daughter was filling all my needs, thank you. Kidding!

Mackenzie has sworn me to secrecy about our meetups, especially from her mother, who told her to avoid me because I'm a commitment-phobe. I wouldn't say that's exactly true. I was with Rayna for a year. She didn't mind my dedication to my career, as she was passionate about her own. It worked. Until it didn't.

Though Rayna often complained I wasn't expressive enough, or was it open enough? I hear that a lot from women, that I'm emotionally distant. Maybe I don't have deep emotions anymore. I had to shut them down or drown. It was them or me.

Deep, true love isn't worth the risk. Dad never recovered from the loss of Mom. His life ended the day she died of ovarian cancer. He lost his job as an architect because he couldn't focus anymore. Now he only leaves the house for work at a warehouse. No friends, no life.

I was a freshman in college when Mom died. I lost her, the Dad I used to know and, a year later, my serious girlfriend Brenda. Car accident. I had to push all that grief into a tiny box to be dealt with later so I could function. And it worked. I graduated college while playing at the top of my game, leading to minor league baseball recruiters scouting me.

And now, after this latest in a series of relationships that ended with me disappointing a woman in the emotional-availability department, I guess I'm at a point in my life where I can accept being alone.

That's what's so great about this casual thing with Mackenzie—there's no pressure, no expectations. A woman who only wants the fun part. Amazing. I don't know why I ever attempted relationships before. This is the way to go.

I pull open the door and breathe in the delicious scent of fresh-roasted coffee. Hailey let me know you get double points on your reward card on Fridays at Something's Brewing Café, but only until ten a.m., so I came over as soon as I could drag myself out of bed.

The café is a warm cozy space with dark wood tables, deep red walls, and golden sconces around hanging lights. I get in line, eyeing the pastries in the glass case while I wait— scones, banana loaf, pain au chocolat, and some intriguing cookie bars with chocolate and cherry. I'm not as strict with my diet now that I don't need to be in top athletic form.

A few minutes later, I take my cappuccino and banana loaf (hey, it has fruit in it) and turn to find a table. I freeze. Mackenzie's sitting with a guy who looks like a damn movie star. Her lips part in surprise. We haven't covered what to do for the random public encounter.

Maybe he is a movie star. Short dark hair, piercing blue eyes, chiseled jaw. Hailey told me that Mackenzie's aunt is Claire Jordan, and Mackenzie's close friends with Shayla Adler. Clearly, she has Hollywood ties.

I clench my teeth, my feet frozen to the ground. Mackenzie can have coffee with any guy she wants. We're the definition of casual.

Nod and be on your way —

To her table.

"Don't you have work today?" Not my smoothest greeting but *come on.*

She gives me a bright smile. "Oh, hi, Cal. I remember you from the Valentine's dance. How's lawyer life?"

So we're playing it that way, huh?

The guy offers his hand. "In case you don't remember, I'm Nathan. I'm sure Hailey and Mackenzie introduced you to a bunch of people that night."

I relax. I remember him now. He was there with a date, not Mackenzie. "Right. Too bad everyone wasn't wearing name tags for my benefit."

He smiles. Mackenzie lets out a high-pitched laugh like she's nervous. Is she afraid I'll spill our dirty little secret? I'd never kiss and tell. Nathan gives her a strange look.

I incline my head. "Good to see you both."

"Have a seat," Nathan says, pushing out the chair across from him with his foot. "We were just wrapping up our meeting."

"Cool." I take a seat. They both stare at me. Nathan's chill, but Mackenzie looks about to bolt. "Was it a business or personal meeting?"

At Mackenzie's widened eyes, I quickly amend, "None of my business."

"New client brief," Nathan says. "We run Brooks Campbell Security along with Owen Campbell, but Mackenzie here is the glue that keeps us together. We've got a complex work situation with two clients—"

Mackenzie cuts him off. "He doesn't want to hear about work stuff. Speaking of work, I should go. Lots to do." She stands.

"Sit a minute with us; then I'll go with you," Nathan says. "I've got some papers I need to give you back at the office."

"Just tell me where they are."

"What's the hurry?"

Me. I'm the hurry. I take a sip of coffee and watch Mackenzie over the rim of my mug. Her cheeks are flushed, and that makes me think of last night, her lusty sigh, the way she reached for me, eager to join.

I look away, pushing lust down. My neck feels hot. Nathan stares at me. Mackenzie takes her seat, and he stares at her, too.

"Something going on with you two?" Nathan asks.

"No," I say at the same time as Mackenzie exclaims, "Don't be silly! We just met!"

The woman is not chill. She may as well announce it—we had sex!

Nathan cocks his head. "Hold up. Did your mom try to set you up with the new single guy in town?"

"Just the opposite," I say. "She warned her away from the player with commitment issues."

Nathan laughs. "Aren't we all? Hey, what was it like to play triple A ball? Was it as cool as it sounds?"

"Playing your favorite sport as a job. Doesn't get any better than that."

"I used to follow the Hartford Yard Goats."

I grin at the funny name. "The Goats. Buddy of mine played shortstop for them before he was called up."

We start talking baseball. That goes on for so long that I finish my coffee and suddenly realize Mackenzie's falling asleep sitting up. Her head rests on her hand, her eyes closing for longer moments. Looks like our late nights are catching up to her.

"I'll let you get back to work." I stand and fish my business card out of my wallet, handing it to Nathan. "Open for business March first. I've got a background in corporate law, but I've been reading up on Gabe's cases to make myself more useful in town."

"Cool. Thanks."

Mackenzie wakes up. "I hope we don't need a lawyer. No offense."

My gaze lingers on Mackenzie's beautiful face. There's something about her eyes—intelligence shines there but also spirit. A pulse beats in her throat. I love to kiss her there and breathe in her sweet scent. I mentally shake it off and force a neutral expression. "I never take offense when someone says no offense."

Nathan laughs. Mackenzie fights a smile.

I lift a palm. "Nice to see you both again."

Mackenzie flashes a bright smile. "Bye! Good luck with everything." She says it like I'm just the new guy in town. No special naked connection.

I leave, the cold winter air a relief after that strange encounter. No way we can keep this thing a secret in a small town for long, and that was the only way she agreed to do anything in the first place. Mostly because her mom warned her away from me for being a player, and Mackenzie doesn't want to deal with her mom's *I told you so*, even though I never was a guy to do casual hookups until Mackenzie, and she came on to me! This is so fucked up. I trudge back toward the inn.

"Cal!" a familiar feminine voice calls.

I turn, my gut tightening at the sight of Mackenzie rushing toward me. I half want to catch her in my arms. "Hey," I say warmly. Now she'll apologize for acting like she barely knows me.

"You forgot your banana bread." She shoves it in my hand. "Bye!"

"Thanks," I say to no one. She already sprinted away.

I continue toward the inn, an uncomfortable feeling gnawing at me. I have no claim on her, so why does it bother me that she pretends I'm some random new guy? Just because we had an amazing hookup followed by five more amazing nights?

It's just that I know how to make her moan and, dammit, it's my name she says over and over. I don't know why that matters, but it does.

I try to shake it off. We're probably only going to keep this up for one more week. That's when I start work. Better timing that way for forgetting her. Two weeks still counts as casual.

My phone chimes with a text.

Mackenzie: *That was too weird. Let's stop this craziness before it gets messy.*

I exhale sharply. Messy? How can things get messy when we agreed it's casual? It's not like it'll complicate things with anyone else since I barely know anyone here. This is just between me and her, which is exactly what I text her.

I have half a mind to turn around, go back to the café, and tell her to her face.

What am I getting so worked up about? This is nothing, a fun whatever. I shove my phone in my pocket, ignoring the chimes of new texts coming in. She can text her lame excuses all day for all I care. We both know she'll show up tonight at midnight.

~

Mackenzie

Day three of not spending the night with Cal. Last night was a nail biter. It's so tempting when he's right across the street and all my traitorous body remembers is the *never-ending pleasure*. The man has skills, I'll give him that.

But casual has its limits, right? Five nights in a week was already far more than I've ever dared for a casual fling. Also, when I texted Cal that we needed to end things, followed up by lots of very good reasons, his response was a big fat nothing. The least he could do is text back OK. Would it have killed him to say he'll miss me but it's for the best? I don't ask for much.

I sip my wine and let the conversation flow around me, only half listening at our regular Sunday night family dinner at my parents' house. It's nice to have cozy family time where I don't have to think about anyone besides my beloved family members—Mom, Dad, Finn, Cooper and now Rowan, Cooper's fiancée. Rowan's smart and hardworking. Her caramel brown hair falls in a shine of silk to her shoulders. It's her natural color too.

Anyway, I love Rowan. She fits right in with our family. So well that Mom made her partner in her wedding planning business. At one time, Mom hoped that would be me, and now that door's closed forever. Mom didn't even ask me if I was okay with it.

I'm really trying to be okay with it. Part of me feels like I was passed over. I push down the uneasy feeling of not living up to expectations that's dogged me my entire life where Mom's concerned.

"It's nice that Cal's getting settled in town," Mom chirps, disturbing my peaceful Cal-free time. "I invited him for dinner tonight—"

"What?" Adrenaline shoots through me. I'm not prepared. I didn't even put on makeup. I have to look like I'm perfectly fine moving on and not thinking of him at all!

Mom sighs. "But he couldn't make it."

I take a slow, deep breath.

She continues, "I didn't want to bring up such a sensitive topic with him, but I hope his ex, Rayna, wasn't spiteful enough to take his stuff before he had a chance to clear out his apartment."

Rayna. I have so many questions about the woman he lived with. I've never lived with any man. I'd have to be serious about them to even consider it because separating your stuff once it's over is more pain than I want to sign up for.

I spear a green bean. "Would she do that?"

Mom finishes chewing a piece of roast beef and dabs her mouth with a napkin. "Breakups can be messy, and a woman scorned and all that. She put in a year of her thirties only to be disappointed with mismatched expectations. I think if you decide to live with someone, it should be clear if it's a situation of convenience, like saving on rent, or a step on the commitment train."

I still, surprised to hear Cal and Rayna were together for a year. That doesn't sound like a commitment-phobe to me. Now that I think about it, they must've been together for a while for her to expect a proposal on Valentine's Day. He bounced back surprisingly fast. Disturbing.

Cooper mouths at me, "Commitment train." I suppress a laugh. Mom always uses funny old-fashioned lingo. I think it's from watching too many black-and-white screwball romantic comedies. Cooper maintains it's her natural personality.

Mom continues, slicing off another bite of roast beef. "Wouldn't it be easier if couples said right up front what they want from a relationship?"

"Like you and I did?" Dad asks, his brown eyes dancing with amusement.

Mom shoots him a dark look. They were the farthest thing from open communicators in the beginning. At one point in their marriage, they went to couples counseling to get better at the whole communication thing. They were very open about it with us kids. Dad still likes to give her a hard time, though to be fair he's like that with everyone. It's his way.

"Absolutely," Rowan says in answer to Mom's question on couples and their expectations. Rowan's blue eyes land on Cooper with total adoration. "That's how I was with Cooper from the beginning. Open and honest."

Cooper inclines his head, neither agreeing nor disagreeing. I don't remember them being all that clear with each other. Wasn't there a huge problem with Rowan going from jilted bride to being "rescued" by my brother? I seem to remember a lot of bumps on that ride.

"Thank you, Rowan," Mom says.

We eat in silence for a few moments. Dad's a great cook.

Finn shoves his brown hair away from his eyes while declaring with a strong and sure voice, "I've been clear with Olivia with expectations and all." Except they're only email pen pals. Olivia lives in LA and travels with my famous friend Shayla Adler as her right-hand woman. Finn's too young for Olivia. He's still in college, but he doesn't care about their four-year age difference. He met her last year, and his romantic poet heart was instantly smitten. Olivia, on the other hand, was baffled as to what in the world he wanted with her. I bet he writes her poems and she tells him about her busy schedule.

"You mean for your email relationship?" Cooper asks Finn.

Finn points his bread at Cooper. "Things can evolve."

Mom smiles. She and Finn share the same romantic tendencies.

Cooper smirks. "Keep emailing her your poetry. I'm sure you'll get there."

Rowan elbows Cooper.

"Ow!"

Rowan gives Finn a sweet smile. "I'm sure Olivia appreciates hearing from you."

After we finish eating dinner, Mom and Dad exchange a silent communication that has me sitting up straighter. Something's up.

"Your dad and I have an announcement," Mom says. "We're doing a vow-renewal ceremony in April, and you're all invited."

"Like a wedding?" I ask.

"A little more low key," Dad says. "It's a romantic way of affirming the relationship."

Mom totally coached him on that. I about die trying not to

laugh. Cooper can't hold it in, and Dad tosses a green bean at him.

"Yes," Mom enthuses. "What could be more romantic than saying I'd marry you all over again? Right, warrior beast?"

"Right, warrior princess," Dad says, his warm gaze radiating love. They set a high bar. Okay, their nicknames are weird, but that's just them.

Mom turns to Rowan. "And it could be a wonderful add-on to our business."

Rowan jumps in enthusiastically. "Weddings, sologamy ceremonies, and vow renewals. We can cover all generations. I love it."

Sologamy is a ceremony where a woman marries herself, pledging a commitment to self-care and love. Guys can do it, too, but so far none have. It's something that Mom's former business partner, Ally, got into, and now it's part of their business.

Mom beams. "Speaking of sologamy, Mackenzie, Rowan, how would you like to have a sologamy ceremony? Maybe with some friends? I'm sure Harper would be on board."

"I'd love to," Rowan says.

Mom claps.

"Sure," I mumble. Rowan's doing it, and it would look bad if I said no. I do want to support Mom's, well, their business now, even if dressing up for a ceremony at a place for weddings isn't really my thing.

Rowan smiles. "I should try out all of our business options."

"We need to get married before we can have a vow renewal," Cooper says.

Rowan cups his jaw and kisses him. "I look forward to it." They're planning a simple justice-of-the-peace ceremony this summer. Some people might find that strange considering she works at the best wedding venue in the area, but it's also where her first wedding was supposed to be held, so it's understandable she wouldn't want to go back to the scene of the crime.

"I'm not sure about Harper," I say. I can't imagine my cousin doing something so touchy-feely as a sologamy ceremony.

"Of course Harper," Mom says. "She's happily single like you. This would just affirm that. You are happily single, aren't you?"

I stiffen, sensing dangerous territory. When Mom gets started on my single status, I throw up a wall. "Yes, of course. Absolutely."

I pour more wine for Mom and then myself. "Speaking of add-ons at work, we have this situation with two clients that could be a conflict of interest. Owen thinks we should drop one of them, but I say why lose the revenue? There has to be a workaround."

"I'm sure you'll figure out an equitable solution," Mom says. "I have faith in you."

"Thanks, Mom."

"Kick some ass," Dad says.

"Josh!" Mom exclaims. She doesn't like curse words, proclaiming them unladylike. Her mom really did a number on her with all the lady rules. I adapt them to suit myself.

The corner of Dad's mouth curls up. "What?"

"Her work isn't a karate studio, and we don't say that word at dinner."

Dad stifles a laugh. He made sure we were all trained blackbelts because he wanted us to kick ass if we needed to. Mom never made it past yellow belt (the first level up) because she didn't like sparring with other people. She worried she'd hurt them. Ha. More like the other way around.

"I believe in you, too," Dad says to me. Then he points to Cooper, Finn, and Rowan in turn. "All of you."

We thank him. He surprises you sometimes with sweetness.

Mom beams. "Me too. All of you. Mackenzie, I could really use your help with the Clover Park Spring Fair this year. We've got a meeting about it with the Chamber of

Commerce on Thursday. Do you think you could make time for it?"

My business is technically part of the Chamber of Commerce, but we don't sell direct to the public. It's not exactly a great use of our resources.

"We're trying to get the younger generation more involved," she says. "The town's future is in your hands. Cooper and Rowan will be there."

Guilt weighs me down—Mom guilt, the future of the town I love, Rowan, the newcomer, jumping in to help, which makes me look bad if I don't. How many things am I going to sign up for because Rowan is doing it? It's not like she can ever take my place as favorite (and only) daughter. Right? Right?!

"I'll be there," I say, pasting on a smile.

Mom beams. "Excellent. This'll be fun."

6

I step into the Clover Park Chamber of Commerce meeting and notice two things at once—Mom gesturing for me to take the seat next to her, and Cal sitting across from her. He seems relaxed and comfortable at what must be his first meeting. *Proceed carefully*. I can't let on that Cal and I had a small fling.

That I can't stop thinking about.

I smile and greet everyone, but most of them don't even notice because they're already arguing about the spring fair, and the meeting hasn't even officially started yet. There's Rachel and Shane O'Hare, who own the book store, café, and ice-cream place in town; Barry Furnukle, the fro-yo shop owner; Tino Garcia, the pizzeria owner; Fran Wilson, the toy store owner; and Armand, the beauty salon owner. Armand is his last name, and he won't share his first name, so don't ask. I bet it's something like Lionel or George and it doesn't go with his cool salon vibe.

Rowan and Cooper aren't here like Mom said they'd be. I feel duped.

Cal's gaze collides with mine, a hint of a smile playing over his lips. My heart thumps harder. He stands, walking over to the side table for coffee.

I drop into the seat next to Mom and whisper, "Where's Cooper and Rowan?"

"Coop had to take a shift at Happy Endings, and Rowan stayed late to wrap up our year-end accounting. She's a wizard with numbers and marketing. I don't know how I got by without her."

I'm a wizard with numbers and marketing. A small sting of betrayal tinges my voice. "I told you I'd take a look at your accounting. I have a degree in it."

She pats my arm. "You've got your own business to take care of."

Did not meet expectations.

I shift my attention, watching Cal as he adds creamer to his coffee, takes a sip, and then adds more.

I keep my voice low. "Why is a lawyer here?" *Are you matchmaking again?*

"Ignore him but be polite."

"If he's not worthy, why keep inviting him to stuff?"

She smiles serenely, taking a pen from her purse and a small notepad. "Because I'm helping him network."

"But you invited him to Sunday dinner too."

"That was also networking. Dad and I are very well connected."

Hmm…good excuses. Possibly not matchmaking?

Cal takes his seat. Mom smiles at him, her eyes sparkling like she thinks he's all that. This is definitely a setup.

Shane hits the gavel twice, and everyone settles down. Despite his age, sixties, his hair is still red with only a tinge of gray on the sides. "Last year's races and events brought in a nice boost to business. This year we want to draw in people not just locally but across the entire state. To do that, I propose we give the fair a name that has something to do with the state of Connecticut."

"Bigger than Clover Park," Mom says, "but centered in Clover Park. Great idea!"

Shane inclines his head.

"Well, it is the nutmeg state," I say. "How about a Nutmeg Festival?"

"Good thought, but another town's already doing that," Shane says.

"How about Nutmeg Pie Festival?" Barry asks. Let's just say Barry often has out-there ideas. His fro-yo shop is called The Dancing Cow, and he's been known to put on a cow costume and dance for customers. I used to feel bad for his daughter, Violet, as a kid—at least my parents had the decency to dance in normal clothes—but now that she's grown up, she joins him sometimes.

"Is that a thing?" Rachel asks. "Nutmeg pie?"

"Can you even eat nutmeg pie?" Mom asks. "Doesn't nutmeg kill you in large quantities?"

Barry points at Mom. "You're thinking of almonds. Cyanide."

Mom's eyes widen. "That can't be. I eat almonds all the time."

Barry pulls out his phone. "Fact check!"

"Later for the fact check," Shane says.

Barry puts his phone down. "The state bird of Connecticut is the American robin." He's big into birds. He even goes on vacations specifically to bird-watch. "Our spring fair could be an American robin festival. That would bring in bird-watchers from all over the East Coast."

"The problem with a bird festival is…" I trail off, sensing Cal's intense stare. Actually it's more a smoldering look, like he's remembering me in the bedroom. I discreetly pull my blouse away from my overheated skin, but it's no use. My body goes into a full meltdown of sexy memories with a tingling that has no right to be there in present company.

"You feeling okay, Mackenzie?" Cal asks in a deep voice like when he spoke in my ear in bed, coaxing more and more pleasure from me.

"This was a bad idea," I say much louder than I mean to. I glance at Mom, who gives me a blank stare. Oh, she's good. Trying to cover up her delight that I'm this affected by the man she put in my path.

Not today, Mom!

I stand. "I need some fresh air."

"But everyone loves birds," Barry says as I'm walking out. "Violet built this cool bird-watching app."

I walk out of town hall and continue briskly down the street. I forgot my coat, but the cool night air feels good after the hot confines of the meeting room. Way too many people in that space. I'm a block away when a familiar voice calls, "Hold up!"

Temptation follows me.

I turn to find Cal approaching, holding my coat and purse. "You forgot these."

"I was coming back."

"Were you?" He helps me put my coat on, which is completely unnecessary, but also weirdly nice.

I face him, determined to power through this little public encounter without giving away my longing, no, my lust for him.

He stands there, searching my expression.

I slide my hair out from under the collar of my coat. "What?"

"What's wrong?"

"Nothing. I just needed some fresh air. It was stifling in there."

"I was comfortable."

"Okay, well, I'll see you in there."

"I'll walk back with you."

It would probably look bad if I sprint ahead of him. We start the walk back.

"You want to get a drink sometime?" he asks.

I swallow hard. "I don't think that's a good idea."

"Why?"

"Because." *Because you're on the rebound. Because I can't bear the heartbreak. Because Mom is secretly trying to manage my love life. I'm almost sure of it.*

"Because why?"

I stop and look at him in the moonlight—his sincere eyes, the familiar bearded line of his jaw, the soft tumble of hair. It's hard to remember why any of the rules matter. "This was supposed to be a onetime thing."

"It was a six-time thing. Well, I guess it depends what you mean by thing. Technically—"

"Let's just go."

"I miss your face."

I stare at him blankly. "You miss my face?"

He gestures around my face, close but not touching. "Like the curve of your cheek when you smile, the way your eyes sort of light up, the way your lips part when you're surprised, like now."

"Cal, as poetic as that is, I think you've mistaken me for a romantic. I'm not. That's why rules and boundaries work for me. Flowers and nice words not so much."

He leans close, bringing a hot rush of desire that nearly makes me grab him. "Is that so?"

"Yes and…" My voice isn't entirely steady. "We had our fun. That part's over."

He dips his head to speak in a gravelly voice near my ear. "The fun part's just beginning."

A hot shiver races down my spine. "Cal."

He shifts, his warm breath a caress on my lips. "Kiss me and tell me you feel nothing."

I grip his coat lapel, not sure if I'm going to shove him away or pull him closer.

He stares at my mouth. My stomach dips, all of my lady parts zinging to life. I know how good this would feel.

I close the distance with a soft kiss to prove him wrong. His hand tangles in my hair, drawing me close as his mouth slants over mine, claiming me. My fingers clutch at his coat, my body swaying close, needing more. Oh God, I missed this.

A siren goes off in the distance, bringing me back to reality. I drop my hold on him, taking a moment to catch my breath. "I felt nothing."

"Right. Same."

"We should get back to the meeting." Just as soon as my legs stop wobbling.

He tips my chin up. "Bye, Mackenzie." Is that longing in his tone?

I start walking in the opposite direction, telling myself I'm doing the right thing. I walk around the block once, twice. I can't walk in with him.

When I get back to the meeting, everyone's packing up. I stand there in a daze. Cal's not here. Is that it? Goodbye forever?

Mom gives me a look of concern. "Are you okay?"

I blink. "Fine. What did we decide on?"

"We're using the state flower as a theme, so now it's the Mountain Laurel Festival hosted by Clover Park. We're having a bulb and flowers sale. I expect we'll draw gardeners from all over the state. They asked if you could contact some master gardeners and the agricultural extension. I'll email you the list."

"Great," I say, turning to go.

"Spring's the time for new beginnings," she says.

Cal's deep voice echoes in my mind. *The fun part's just beginning.*

I force a neutral expression, though I'm dying to find Cal and ask him exactly what he meant by that. Friends with benefits or something more? I was too rattled in the moment to even consider what he was proposing. I turn back and wave bye to Mom.

"And spring's right around the corner," Mom chirps, giving me a sweet smile.

She's definitely acting weird.

∼

Cal

I'm not sure why I'm at Happy Endings bar for Ally's bon voyage party. Ally is Hailey's former business partner, and she's about to cruise around the world with her husband. I mean, sure, Hailey invited me for networking reasons, but I've already been to a couple of these networking events, and I do have a small client list from Gabe. It's a whole lot of Mackenzie's family and honorary family here.

Truth is, I haven't been able to stop thinking about that kiss two days ago. She's not here. What the hell am I doing? Longing for a woman when I know it'll end with her getting hurt. I'm not cut out for relationships, and she was very clear she only wanted casual. But does that mean casual has to end so soon?

This is a mutual hang-up. Once we get each other out of our systems, I'll get back to work mode, and she can do the same.

There's a few tables full of appetizers and a bon voyage sheet cake with a cruise ship made of sugar. I'll stay until they cut the cake, and this will be the last invite from Hailey I accept. Too many reminders of—

Mackenzie. The blood rushes through my veins. All the sights and sounds of the party fade into the background. She's smiling her warm smile as she talks to one of her many cousins and takes off her coat.

Her long brown hair is a soft wave over her shoulders, her skin glowing, her lips lush and pink. Her clothes match her personality—a soft fuzzy pink sweater with leather pants. Soft and sweet but tough. Strong. So sexy.

I lift a hand in a casual greeting, which she doesn't see. Another of her many cousins steps in front of her. I can't keep track of this family. There's biological and honorary aunts, uncles, and cousins along with two younger brothers. You'd think it would be easy to pick out who was who, but there's a lot of family resemblance going on with her dad and uncle being identical twins.

My gaze follows her as she greets people. Our nights together were a thrill right up there with a home run. Just seeing her gets my adrenaline going, like I'm up to bat, all eyes on me. The anticipation—will it be the thrill of a hit, or the whoosh of a swing and miss?

It is not one-sided. That kiss made her melt into me. I run a hand through my hair. What will it take to get her out of my system?

She's at the bar now. The bartender smiles and jokes with her. That's Cooper, her younger brother and heir apparent to the Happy Endings bar. I weave my way through the crowd to her.

I'm nearly there when a man blocks my way. I didn't even hear him coming. Stealth mode. It's Mackenzie's dad, Josh. His dark hair is rumpled, dress casual, but his stance is anything but. The man looks lethal. Didn't Hailey mention something about Josh being a paratrooper in the Army? Those guys are trained in hand-to-hand combat.

"How's it going?" he asks.

I straighten my spine. "Good." I can't help it; I glance over his shoulder as Mackenzie greets someone with a hug.

"Eyes here," he commands. "Settling into your new job?"

I meet his eyes. "Yes, thanks." His tone has me on edge like I'm in dangerous territory, but I have no idea how I got here.

"What's going on between you and my daughter?"

Did Mackenzie say something about me?

"Uh…"

"My wife saw you in the street during the Chamber of Commerce meeting."

Hailey saw us kiss? Or was it the intense conversation before that?

I swallow hard and lift my palms. "Just friends."

"Appreciate the intel."

I nearly salute, but I fear he'd take it wrong and knock me flat on my ass. Was that a warning, or was he just in overprotective dad mode?

I turn to find a smiling Hailey behind me. Did she hear all that?

"How's everything?" she asks brightly.

"Couldn't be better," Josh says, his entire demeanor changing as he turns to face his wife.

"I'm going to go," I say.

"Oh, not yet," Hailey says. "I want you to meet my sister-in-law Mad Shaw. She's a real estate mogul, mostly residential, but she'd like to get into commercial properties. I think you could help each other out. Sales and legal contracts go together."

Seems like Hailey really wants me to succeed in my new law practice. I appreciate that. I follow her to Mad, a woman with short brown hair and a fierce expression that reminds me of Josh. She must be his sister. Before I can introduce myself, Mad says to Hailey, "So this is the guy?"

"This is him," Hailey says proudly.

My head's spinning. *Am I the enemy or the hero in this strange family?*

Mad gives me a once-over. "I get it. Harvard law too. Not too shabby. What're you doing in a small town like this?"

I give my usual answer, grew up in a small town, tired of the city. I sense someone staring and catch Mackenzie's eye. She gives me a small wave. Relief rushes through me. She's not avoiding me after our sidewalk kiss. I don't know what came over me when I did that. She's like a sizzling pitch I have to catch and fire back and...she's giving me a concerned look.

I lift a hand.

She mouths, "Sorry."

Sorry for her dad ambushing me? Sorry for ending things when clearly there's still chemistry? Eventually it'll fizzle out, but right now it's like a living, breathing thing between us.

She pulls out her phone and texts. My phone vibrates in my pocket. I'm dying to check it, but Mad and Hailey are talking to me. Wait, it's quiet. Did they ask me a question?

"Can you repeat that?" I ask.

"I don't think he's serious," Mad says.

Hailey smiles and pats my arm. "He's just a little distracted. It's a party."

"I'm serious," I say. "What're we talking about?"

Mad fills me in. "I want to help the town buy the old Fagan property and turn it into a community recreation center. The old man lives at his son's house halfway across the country now, so he's game. Would you ever take in a parent?"

I'm momentarily thrown by the sudden change of topic. I clear my throat. "Mom died when I was a freshman in college. Dad never wants to leave the house where they lived together, so I guess I'd say no. Probably wouldn't come up." I push the grief back into its box buried deep inside me.

"Oh no, I'm so sorry," Hailey says. "I hope she didn't suffer. What happened?"

"You can't ask that," Mad says.

"Why not?" Hailey asks.

"Because it's personal," Mad says through her teeth.

Hailey turns to me. "Cal and I have gotten to know each other pretty well, right, Cal?"

"You've shared a lot," I say diplomatically.

"See?" Mad says. "You shared. Not him. Let's get back to business."

Mackenzie appears, placing a hand on my arm. Warmth rises from the small touch and spreads through me. I really miss her touch. "Can I steal him away?"

Mad and Hailey exchange a look I can't interpret.

"Mad, I'd be happy to help with any legal contracts," I say. "Nice to meet you."

I follow Mackenzie to the back room of the restaurant. She stops by a jukebox, puts a quarter in, and runs her finger along the selections.

"Thanks for the save," I say.

She keeps her eyes on the jukebox. "You looked cornered."

"They were asking about my deceased mother."

She turns to me, eyes wide. "Oh my God. Unacceptable. And I'm sorry. Sutton mentioned it before. I understand how hard it must be." Her lips form a flat line. "You know what?

I'm going to have a talk with them. Was it Mom or Aunt Mad who brought it up?"

"I don't want to cause a problem for you."

"It's my problem already." She jabs a button, and a Tom Petty song starts. She turns to go, but I stop her with a hand on her shoulder. She stiffens. I drop my hand, stung by the rejection.

"Don't worry about it," I say. "I'm fine."

"Okay." She gestures for me to follow her to a small table in a corner of the room. I take the seat opposite her. "So, Cal, I have to ask, how'd you get roped into another Campbell family gathering?"

I lean forward. "Networking."

She narrows her eyes. "So you're going to keep showing up to all business and personal events organized by my mother?"

"Depends."

"On what?"

"Will you be there?"

"Cal."

"Mackenzie."

"It's not that I don't like you. I do. Very much."

My heart shifts in my chest, a weird feeling. I hope it's okay in there. "So?"

"I just think *us* is a bad idea. You're on the rebound. We're both not into commitment—"

"Who said anything about commitment?"

"Oh."

"Your dad was asking what the deal was with us."

Her jaw drops.

"I told him we were just friends, and I think that was the right answer." I glance around, suddenly wary. I should know where Josh is at all times in relation to his daughter. "He sounded lethal."

She crinkles her nose, thinking for a moment. "Well, he is, but he doesn't usually get involved with guys I know. That's so strange."

"I wouldn't know. I only met him once before."

She stills, staring across the room. I follow her gaze to where Hailey and Mad watch us as they casually sip drinks. Mackenzie huffs. Hailey and Mad suddenly get into an intense conversation.

"Mom put him up to it," she says.

I swallow hard, thinking about how Hailey warned Mackenzie away from me. "I guess she doesn't see me as good enough for her daughter."

She cocks her head, pursing her lips. "Or maybe she thinks you're perfect for me."

"I don't think that's it."

"She told me to be polite, but she's hoping for more than politeness."

"That doesn't make sense."

Her expression turns fierce, reminding me a little of her dad. Do *not* want to get on her bad side. Maybe this whole pushing for more time with her was a bad idea. I decide to lay it all out there.

"I'm not good at relationships. I'm too closed off." I search my memory for all the ways I've disappointed women. "Emotionally unavailable, a workaholic, and a commitment-phobe."

She lifts a finger. "Except for when you lived with someone for a year."

"We were together for a year, but we only lived together for a few months, and that was only because her lease ran out and my roommate left. It was a temporary arrangement."

"Hmm."

"Really. We talked about it ahead of time." I leave out how bad things got after she moved in. She doesn't need to hear all the gory details.

She pats my arm. "It's okay. I don't judge you for being confused about your relationship. Men often are."

"I'm not—"

She gestures airily. "Obviously you're not marriage material, being on the rebound, so what's Mom really hoping for?"

"I don't think she's hoping for anything."

"Everyone makes a big deal of the whole proposal and wedding deal. I say what's the rush to tie yourself to someone for the rest of your life? Anyway, the kind of lasting love my parents have is rare."

I'm getting dizzy from the topic changes around here. Is there a point to this? I don't dare ask.

I lean in. "Does this mean you and I can't…because we don't have what your parents have?"

"Don't be ridiculous," she says quickly. Too quickly.

I lean back, understanding dawning. "I get it now. You say you want casual, but you really don't."

"I want casual, which by definition is brief. Like what we had. I mean, in the past, not to be repeated."

"You don't want what your parents have, trust me."

"I don't?"

"No. My parents were high school sweethearts. Dad's still not over her, and it's been fifteen years since Mom died. He still has all her clothes in the closet, everything in the house right where she left it. He lost his job because he couldn't focus anymore. He was an architect. He never leaves the house except for his warehouse job. It's like he stopped living when he lost her."

"Oh, that's so sad."

I let out a breath, pushing the darkness back into its box. "Yeah."

"Still, I can't keep accidentally-on-purpose running into you at family and town events. It makes her feel like she's winning."

"Winning what?"

She starts texting. "Watch this." She shows me the message: *You were right. Cal's a major commitment-phobe. Doesn't even want to be friends anymore.*

Mom: *I'm so relieved. Just asking for heartache.*

She gives me a pointed look. "See? Matchmaking."

"I don't get it."

"You will. I'm going to take care of this once and for all. Stay here."

"Oh-kay."

She walks away with a determined look in her eye. Are they about to have a public battle over me? Will her dad kick my ass afterward? He wasn't exactly warm and fuzzy tonight.

I get the feeling a storm's about to crash through my life courtesy of Mackenzie. I've never felt more alive.

7

Mackenzie

Mom and I head to Dad's office in the back of Happy Endings for a private talk. As soon as I shut the door behind us, she says, "What's wrong?"

I take a steadying breath. I don't want to lash out in anger over her meddling ways. I'm a mature adult. No curse words necessary *this time*. "Mom, I get the feeling you're doing a little matchmaking between me and Cal."

Her eyes widen. "Why do you say that? I told you to stay away from him. The man clearly has commitment issues."

"Yes, but then you invited him to the Chamber of Commerce meeting."

She smiles. "So? He should be part of town events. He's the town lawyer now."

"The same meeting you invited me to for the first time."

"A long overdue invitation."

I huff, my temper spiking. It's very hard to hold my temper in the face of her serene replies. I understand why Dad was driven to an escalating prank war with her back in the day. "Bit of a coincidence, the timing, don't you think?"

She lifts one shoulder in a dainty shrug. "Is that all? I'd like to get back to the party. Ally's going away for four months, so I want to spend more time with her. Me and the girls planned a fun dance to surprise her with. Come on, let's go."

I hold up a palm. "Wait. I think it's suspicious that you keep inviting Cal to stuff where you know I'll be. Like this party."

She shakes her head. "Not everything's about you, Mackenzie. There's lots of other people at these events. I'm just trying to make him feel welcome in his new hometown. I'd want someone to do the same for you if you moved to a new town."

"What's with all the networking help?" I ask in complete exasperation.

"If he doesn't have enough work, we'll lose our town lawyer."

In the face of her extreme denial and reasonable explanations, I'm forced to give up the fight. "Okay, but under no circumstances are you to matchmake me with anyone ever again. You made a solemn promise to Dad to stop. I have no problem ratting you out, and he will *not* be happy."

Mom loves to make Dad happy and is miserable if he's upset with her, which he rarely is. Have to say, the reverse is also true. #couplegoals

She flips her strawberry-blonde hair over her shoulder and opens the door. "Dad will have no reason to be unhappy with me. Try to mingle with some other guys, Mackenzie. Cal's a dead end in the romance department."

I stand there for a moment. Maybe she's right about Cal, and she's been looking out for me all along. I smooth my hair back and try to think this through. Is it me? Maybe I'm being paranoid because of her past matchmaking efforts on my behalf. Not to mention the Mom matchmaking stories from my aunts, uncles, and her friends. Legendary. Subtle. *Persistent*. Aunt Lauren even signed up for her Make Love Bloom™ plan, which Mom trademarked and everything. The plan fell flat on its face, but Aunt Lauren ended up with the love of her life *despite it*. Mom still takes credit, saying she helped Aunt Lauren see what was out there and to appreciate what was right in front of her. Who can argue with that kind of logic?

I feel a little silly now. I can't let the past warp my view of reality.

I make a right onto my parents' street. It's Saturday, a week after my talk with Mom, and I offered to help her out with a trip to an estate sale. I haven't run into Cal all week, so that's the end of that.

Okay, hard truth—I've spent way too much time thinking about the wisdom of getting involved with a guy who casually leaves a year-long relationship. As if getting involved with Cal is a real problem I have. He's shown no signs of wanting to be further involved with me. Not even a text.

I miss him. I wish that weren't true.

Maybe Cal realized late that he and Rayna weren't right for each other. Or does he really have a problem with commitment? Would he leave me if we got serious? I know there's no way of knowing a relationship is a sure thing, but I'd like some assurances if I was going to venture in that direction. Some way of knowing that there's something special between us. A sign. That sounds ridiculously superstitious and borderline romantic.

Obviously great sex has made me delusional. The man told me he's bad at relationships. I need to believe him.

And stop thinking about him.

And fantasizing about him.

Life goes on, right? One foot in front of the other. Speaking of which, Mom sprained her ankle attempting pickleball with her friends. I feel bad for her, but at the same time it's a well-known fact that dodging the ball only works in dodgeball.

Parking in my parents' driveway, I brace myself for a long day. I'm going to drive Mom to an estate sale in the country, where she plans to bid on some antiques for Ludbury House. She's always on the lookout for antique furniture and wedding gear like candlesticks, vases, and tablecloths for her wedding planning office and venue.

I ring the bell and wait. I've got a key, but you never know when a horny parent will decide to take advantage of an empty nest and go for a living room romp. Seriously don't want to see that. Again.

Mom answers the door on crutches, wearing a purple dress, a loafer, and an ankle boot. She still looks radiant. She shifts back to let me in. "Thank you so much for coming! I appreciate you helping me out on your day off."

"Of course. What were you thinking with a ball sport?"

"Aunt Mad convinced me pickleball was easy. She said it was like Ping-Pong." She gives me a *can you believe it* look.

"Not so much."

"No."

"Shouldn't you be off your feet? Where's Dad?"

"I had my ankle elevated all morning. I've been up since five. And Dad's making pancakes. Want some?"

"I'm good. Already ate."

Dad appears wearing an apron and holding a spatula. "I made banana chocolate-chip."

My favorite. My mouth waters. "With crushed walnuts on top and homemade whipped cream?"

Dad smirks. "Is there any other way?"

Calories be damned! "Okay, one pancake."

"Great!" Mom says. "Take your time. I don't need to be first for browsing the antiques. I've catalogued what I want from the website. The auction's not until twelve."

I step into the kitchen, where a place is already set for me. Dad serves me up a fluffy pancake, sprinkles walnuts on top, ladles on a generous dollop of whipped cream, and indicates the maple syrup nearby.

The first bite is heaven. Truth is, nothing beats Dad's cooking. He's been taking classes for years and loves experimenting in the kitchen. We're so spoiled; even restaurant cooking can't compare. Other than Dad's restaurant, of course.

"So good," I say. This almost makes up for spending my Saturday shopping for antiques. I much prefer a modern style in home decor.

Dad smiles and goes back to making more pancakes.

"Who's going to eat all these pancakes?" I ask, thinking my brothers may have gotten roped into antique shopping, too.

Mom sits at the table, setting her crutches next to her. "We'll have leftovers all week for breakfast, and Cooper pops in regularly."

I cut another piece of pancake and distribute walnuts, whipped cream, and syrup on top. "So, Dad, not into estate sale shopping?" I take a bite of pancake heaven. Too bad I had a breakfast smoothie, or I could eat more of these.

Dad turns from the stove. "I've got an event at Happy Endings later this afternoon. Can't fit in the long drive."

"So you're buttering me up with pancakes."

"Nah. Just wanted to make my favorite daughter happy."

I roll my eyes, even though I'm secretly delighted. "I'm your only daughter."

"Still my favorite one."

I shake my head, smiling. The doorbell rings. "Can Cooper smell pancakes across town?"

Mom and Dad exchange a look that sets my nerves on edge. Mom's look says *be chill*, and Dad's says *You didn't*. Uh-oh.

"I'll get it," Dad says, turning off the stovetop. "Just finished in time."

Mom gives me an apologetic smile. "I asked Cal to come along to do the heavy lifting. There's an antique buffet up for auction I really want for the dining room at Ludbury House. I didn't want you to strain your back, and I'm in no shape to help with this ankle."

My jaw drops. The *audacity*. Pretending to be innocent when I confronted her about matchmaking with Cal and now this.

Oh, it is on.

Cal appears in the kitchen, his large frame sucking all the air from the room. I swear the kitchen feels smaller. "Good morning. I heard there were pancakes."

"Help yourself," Dad says, gesturing to the stack on the counter.

"Thank you." Cal glances at me, says a quick hi, and then goes for the pancakes. He puts two loaded pancakes on a plate and sits next to me, across from Mom.

Mom smiles like she's won the lottery. "Cal, thank you so much for helping out. We really appreciate it."

He chews and swallows his pancake. "Happy to help out. You've done so much for me. I got another new client thanks to you. Mel asked me to help him with that property-line issue."

"Wonderful!" Mom says.

I get why Mom invited him, devious woman, but why did Cal go along with giving up his Saturday? Surely he has a lot to do setting up his new business and apartment. Is he here to appease the woman who's helped him meet everyone in town or to see me? I focus on my pancakes, my mind whirling with what all this means.

"Thank you two so much," Mom says, slowly rising from her chair. Dad rushes to help her, making sure she's all set with the crutches. "Enjoy your pancakes. I'd better go upstairs and raise this ankle. Josh, when you're done in here, join me upstairs."

Dad comes to full attention, whipping off his apron. Mom giggles as he closes the distance, a predatory look in his eyes before he sweeps her off her feet. The crutches clatter to the floor. He carries her out, and Mom wiggles her fingers at us.

I glance sideways at Cal, both embarrassed and happy for them.

He grins.

~

Cal

I head out the door with Mackenzie, who's unusually quiet. She seemed surprised to see me today considering her mom told me that Mackenzie wanted my help. Not that it matters. Mackenzie and I are done. This is just one of those small-town favors people do for each other.

She unlocks her dad's pickup truck and climbs in the driver's side. After I get in, she programs the GPS and then looks at me solemnly. "Doesn't it bother you being a work-horse on a Saturday?"

"I don't mind helping you out."

"Helping *me* out?"

"Yeah, your mom said you wanted my help."

Her lips purse. "Hmm." She backs out of the driveway. "I have a plan. Well, I *will* have a plan."

"You know some back roads?"

"Yes, but that's not what I meant." She bangs on the steering wheel. "It's so obvious I can't believe I fell for her faux surprise."

"Faux surprise? You mean from your mom? When?"

"Who else? And the denial! Ugh. I should've known when she warned me off you the first time we met. Why say I should stay away from you unless she wanted me to do the opposite? She probably counted on my dry spell. Oh, that is so wrong. And then they sent us to Happy Endings to put the catering dishes away. She wanted us to hook up in that closet."

"What!"

She shakes her head. "My aunts warned me that one day I'd be caught in her matchmaking web, but I wouldn't know it until it was too late. So devious. So subtle. If I wanted her matchmaking, I would've joined the club!"

"I'm lost. What club?"

She glances at me before making a turn. "It's a long story. Basically, Mom started the Happy Endings Book Club as a way to matchmake all of her friends, which would ultimately lead to a thriving wedding planning business."

"Matchmaking for work?"

"Oh, it was subtle, persistent but subtle. From what I heard, only women showed up to the book club, and it became a solid friend group."

"Cool."

She presses her lips into a flat line. "That's what they thought, but she was still working in the background. Joke's on her because every single friend found the love of their life before she did. Dad was there the whole time right under her nose, but neither of them could see what they had until her mom married his dad."

I cock my head at the implications. "Your parents are step-brother and stepsister?"

"It's not gross like that. They were already out of the house, around our age—oh, now it makes even more sense. I'm the age she was. You're the age—"

"Me?"

She stops at a traffic light and looks at me, an unholy gleam in her eyes. "Here's the plan. We'll pretend to have a serious relationship to get Mom to admit she's happy we're together, which will expose her devious matchmaking."

"I can't lie to your mom."

"Not lie exactly. We'll go out together in public. She'll just draw the wrong conclusion. Subtle, see? Like her matchmaking. And then I'll catch her in the act, rat her out to Dad, and this will never be a problem again."

"Weren't you all about keeping things between us a secret?"

"That only applied for our one-night stand. Discretion in a small town, not wanting to deal with Mom's I told you so."

"More like six-night—"

"She way overstepped. Cal, she made me think I was being paranoid."

I keep my mouth shut, even though she sounds a wee bit paranoid.

She continues, "Look, I love my weird mom, but she has a long history of matchmaking, foisted some completely unhinged candidates on me in the past, and even after making a solemn promise to my dad that she'd never do it again, she did. With you! So here we are. Are you in?"

Hmm, fake public dating doesn't sound very fun. And won't her parents be mad that we faked them out? I don't need to make enemies in my new adopted town. I've got a law practice to keep afloat.

I attempt to reason with her. "Your mom warned you away from me because she thought I wasn't good enough for you—"

She squeezes my arm. "You're plenty good enough."

My chest puffs out. It's kinda nice to hear. But let's be logical.

"Won't our serious relationship make her mad?" I ask.

"If it does, then we'll end the pretend relationship. If it doesn't, then I'll call her on her matchmaking. She hates to upset Dad, and he takes solemn promises seriously. It's a matter of honor. Here's what we'll do—"

"Hold on." I let the solemn-promise-to-Dad thing slide, even though the lawyer in me thinks she should've had that solemn promise made directly to her. Instead I focus on an advantageous loophole. "What do I get out of this pretend serious relationship?"

"No sex."

"Did I say sex?"

"No sex."

"Damn." *I miss you.* Ah, hell. I do miss her. And it's not just about sex, but at the same time I miss that part too.

Sometimes I dream about her, which I will admit only if she admits she misses me because pride. I have some.

She turns onto the highway and accelerates at a moderate pace. She drives cautiously. I get the feeling that's how she lives her life. Except for the night of our first hookup when she peeled out of the parking lot, I'm guessing due to her eagerness to be with me. I smile to myself. That was a wild night. My mind drifts once again to the moment her dress fell to the floor.

"Here's what you'll get out of it," she says.

I snap back to reality. "Yeah?"

"I'll pay for our dates and throw in one Sunday family dinner so you can have more of Dad's cooking. I'll ask him to make his famous beef stew with fresh-baked sourdough. It's to die for."

"I don't need you to pay, and as much as I like good food, this isn't about seeing more of your family. Your mom invites me to Sunday dinner every week."

"See?"

I go in for the big win. "This plan hinges on us being seen together in public, but I don't think that will prove anything. Everyone will think we're just friends. Hailey's daughter showing the new guy around town."

She's quiet for a moment.

Victory lap coming up. Never negotiate with a lawyer.

"Okay," she says, "we'll have *some* public displays of affection."

"Are we talking three, four gestures per date? Give me the scope of *some*."

She smiles. "You really sound like a lawyer."

"Thank you."

"I went on a date with a lawyer I met in a bar once. He was so-o-o boring."

I'm sensing an insult here, so I go on the offensive. "Seeing as how we already hooked up, I don't think the affection thing will work." *I'll want more.*

"Why not? It's easy—hold hands, arm around the shoulders, just smile at me a lot, okay? And I'll gaze at you like you set the moon."

"So no kissing."

"Probably best not to, don't you think?"

She's awfully cheerful about not kissing me considering she was all over me in bed for a week. And very enthusiastic about it, too. My pride dwindles a bit. I really would like to at least kiss her.

"I think this sounds like a terrible plan." A torturous, terrible plan. Before I can figure out how to request time spent with her in a non-fake way on a few occasions, not too many, but some, she ups the ante.

"I'll help bring your sister to town to work for me, thereby ending her bad relationship."

"Hmm." I hate to admit it, but I've failed Sutton for years, letting her stagnate. All she does is take care of Dad, work, and take whatever scraps of time her stupid boyfriend spares for her.

Mackenzie smiles like she knows she's won. "And that'll also be nice for you to have family in town. I've been wanting to bring Sutton into a larger role for a while now but not while she's remote."

Sutton idolizes Mackenzie as a businesswoman. It could be good for Sutton. And I wouldn't mind having her around. She idolizes me too.

I take a moment to admire Mackenzie in profile while she passes a slow car, from her cute upturned nose to her soft cheek, long hair, and her sexy body in a snug sweater and jeans. She's so beautiful.

I put on my most casual tone. "Okay, but I'd like to put kissing back on the table. It's only natural in a couple." And my kisses have been known to melt this woman into a puddle of aching need. It'd be nice if I wasn't the only one dealing with aching need.

She purses her lips, considering. "Okay, but only in public. Also, I'll touch you frequently, and your job is to enjoy it and not reciprocate."

"You seem to have mistaken me for a eunuch."

"A what?"

"Not having—never mind. Look, I'm all for you touching me wherever and whenever, but you can't expect me not to reciprocate. I'm not dead. Understand?"

She gives me a sideways glance. "You want sex?"

"I want reciprocation."

"Private reciprocation."

"Public's fine." *If that's what you're into.*

She's quiet again. I can almost hear the wheels turning in her brain.

I lower my voice to a husky tone that usually gets results. "Mackenzie, am I free to reciprocate touching frequently?"

"Mmm…yes."

"Then I agree to your terms."

"I can see why you became a lawyer." She powers down her window. "I'm so hot. Isn't it hot in here?"

I hide a smile. "Sure."

She turns the vents toward her and shifts the heat to cool.

Aw, hell. Pride be damned. "I've missed you," I admit.

"In your bed."

"In general."

She powers the window back up. "You only knew me in your bed. Just be honest."

I clamp my mouth shut because I'm dangerously close to admitting how much I think about her—too much—and trying to argue that we're good together. Somehow the more she pushes me away, the more I realize how much I want to be with her. Is it the chase? I've never been so off balance with a woman.

"It's just a game, Cal, okay?" Her voice rises to a panicky pitch. "Can you play the game? If not, we should shut this down right now."

Easy. Take it slow. I recognize that panic. It's the moment before you bail. Been there. "I can play the game."

"Good."

For now. She has no idea about my competitive streak. I play to win.

8

Mackenzie

I may have made a mistake. It's one thing to play couple in public with Cal, it's a whole different ball game to resist him in private. Look how he's already made me think in terms of baseball metaphors!

First, as soon as we parked at the estate sale, he jumped out of the truck, ran around and opened my door, and then helped me out of the truck. His big hands on my waist, his soulful dark eyes smoldering into mine.

And now his hand is burning a hole through my thin coat as he rests it on the small of my back, guiding me down the front path of the mansion hosting the estate sale. Cal has slipped into gallant courtship mode, catching me completely off guard. We're not even in town where anyone I know could witness it and report back to Mom.

His deep voice resonates close to my ear. "This is my first estate sale. Be gentle."

The man is *trying* to get me worked up. I know his game. Fake dating, real sex. Not gonna happen. "Ha! These things can be fun, like a treasure hunt."

He opens the door of the mansion and gestures for me to go ahead. I walk inside, and he helps me out of my coat, folding it neatly over his arm. This courtship business is too much and not what we agreed to. His lawyer side is really showing itself clearly now, always bending the rules and looking for loopholes.

I can't trust him.

He did say he missed me. But I can't risk him casually walking away like he did with his live-in girlfriend. I bet she was *crushed* thinking she was getting a marriage proposal and then nothing. No, thank you.

"Cal."

"Hmm?" He's looking around, taking in the antiques for sale and the variety of numbered items for auction.

"You don't have to do all this stuff for me."

His gaze locks on mine, making my throat go dry and somehow bringing more heat to my already overheated body. "What stuff?"

I play with my hair, suddenly nervous. "You know, like opening doors and helping with my coat and stuff."

"I do that with the person I'm dating. If you want this to look real, I have to start rehearsing so it comes naturally."

I gesture vaguely. "It feels like mixed signals."

He leans down to my ear, lowering his voice to a husky whisper that sends a hot shiver down my spine. "You know what's a mixed signal? Hooking up with someone, ending things, and then pretending to date them."

I shift away. "Sorry. I messed this up, didn't I? You don't have to go through with my wacky scheme."

He tucks a lock of my hair behind my ear. "Nah. Mixed signals are fun. I told you I'm game. Try to keep up."

He walks over to a program sign, holding his phone up to the QR code, which links to the auction program. "Budget?"

"I've got her business credit card. I'll text her as the bid gets higher, and we'll see."

He studies me for so long I start to wonder if I have pancake crumbs on my face. "You don't look much like your mom."

"No kidding."

"But you have the same spark in your eye. Like you're up

for the challenge, whatever it is. I bet you butted heads when you were a kid."

"Actually, I tried to follow in her footsteps to win scholarship money in beauty pageants. Nope. Despite her coaching, I never even placed as a finalist. I couldn't even get Miss Congeniality, and I worked very hard to be a smiley person."

Most people laugh at that. Pageants are silly. Who cares? But Mom and I took it very seriously, and it hurt. Mostly it hurt because I disappointed her.

Cal doesn't laugh. "You're very congenial."

I can't help but notice he didn't say you're so beautiful you should've won. Le sigh.

"Thank you. She tried not to look disappointed, but I could tell she was. That's when I realized I had to forge my own path."

"Never a bad thing. Dad wanted me to be the ball player he always wished he could be. He played in college but didn't make it to the professional level. He barely spoke to me for years after I dropped out of the league."

"I'm sorry."

"We get along better now. Me and Sutton are all he has. Hey, look, free champagne."

We get champagne and do our browsing through the mansion. I take pictures of the china cabinet and buffet set Mom said she wanted to be sure I have the right items. I even measure them for her with an app on my phone.

Cal sticks close to my side, almost but not quite touching. It's *torture*. It would be so easy to tumble into bed with this man, but then what?

What happens after the fun part?

By the time the auction begins, I'm starting to get used to having him close. It makes me feel like we're a couple. We're sitting side by side, his muscular arm resting on the chair behind my back. It's hot as hell.

He raises my paddle for me because apparently I was thinking so much about his arm and the couple thing that I forgot to bid on the item we came here to bid on.

I jerk my wrist from his grip, embarrassed. "I got it."

The numbers climb quickly. I text Mom during the bidding, but it goes so fast I have to stop texting. And then I bid, and it tops out. *Uh-oh*. Four thousand dollars. That's a lot for a china cabinet and buffet to be featured in the dining room of Ludbury House. They don't even have wedding ceremonies in there.

I text her the final bid. "Sorry. I'll cover some."

Mom: *It's fine. I'm planning some lovely pre-sologamy ceremony dinners in there. Just another meaningful add-on! Rowan's arranged some killer PR for it.*

That's Rowan's background—public relations and marketing. Of course she's the better choice to partner with Mom in her business. I push down the hurt.

"You okay?" Cal asks.

He's surprisingly in tune to my moods. I paste on a smile. "Yeah. We got what we came for. Let's go to the staging area. I'll sign the paperwork and pay. You bring the truck around back, and we'll load it up."

"I'll load it up. That's what I'm here for. You want to get some dinner after?"

"No, thanks. Let's just get back."

He searches my expression. "You seem upset."

"I'm fine."

"I'm a good listener."

I shake my head. "Let's go."

Cal

Mackenzie's mood flatlined as soon as the auction ended. She even asked me to drive the truck back to Ludbury House. I glance over at her in the passenger seat, where she's staring out the window. I decide to take a sideways approach in an attempt to get an answer beyond "fine."

"I've been thinking about your offer to get Sutton out here," I say.

"Mmm-hmm."

"What if she doesn't go for it?"

"I can be very convincing. Plus we'll offer a pay bump, three weeks paid time off, and half-day Fridays in the summer."

"Wow. Can I work for you?"

That earns me a smile.

"And how will you convince people we're fake dating?" I ask. "Drinks at your dad's bar?"

She whips out her phone, a spark of her usual energy returning. "I'm looking up the perfect town events we can show up for, where someone bound to know Mom will see us there. She won't be going to a lot of events herself while she's in an ankle boot. She'll want to save her energy for her weddings."

"Did I really agree to this shaky scheme? Who's going to believe it?"

"Everyone. And it's not shaky. I'm the ultimate planner."

"Maybe you should've gone into wedding planning with your mom."

She frowns, her light instantly dimming. "She wanted me to at one point, but I wanted to try my own business, and now it's too late because she brought Rowan in as partner."

"And you wish it were you?"

"I don't know." She sighs. "Rowan's great. It's just Mom never asked me about making Rowan partner. She assumed that door was closed forever for me, and now I guess it is."

"I'm sure she'd make room for you if you really wanted it. Like if your Mom retires, then she could have you and Rowan be partners."

She bites her nail.

"Or not."

I pull onto the highway. Mackenzie's quiet. I'm about to turn on some music when she says in a rush, "Truth is, when Mom first asked me about joining her in the business after college, I didn't think I could live up to her expectations. She's brilliant with people and business. Now Rowan will be the success in Mom's eyes. Forget it. Who cares, right? I've got my thing. I don't know why I unloaded on you."

"But you like your business, right?"

"I do." She lets out a mirthless laugh. "Guess I have some Mom issues. Who doesn't?"

The usual pang of loss hits whenever I think of Mom. "Uh…"

"Shit! I'm sorry. It must be hard to be reminded of your mom. And here I am complaining about mine. Sorry."

"Not my favorite subject."

She reaches over and gives my arm a squeeze. I glance at her, and she gives me a gentle smile. My throat tightens. Her comfort means more than a thousand platitudes about Mom being in a better place. It's been years, but the loss sticks with you.

She turns on the radio. I appreciate her not pushing for the details on Mom's death. A lot of people ask out of their own curiosity, and it's not easy for me to talk about.

"I appreciate you, Mackenzie."

"Why?"

"For being you."

She smiles. "I appreciate you, too, Cal."

I change the subject to a neutral one, movies. Soon we're in a heated debate over whether *Bull Durham* is in fact a baseball movie. Hint: it's not. It's a relationship movie set in the world of baseball. She's a lot of fun to debate with.

Mackenzie has the code for Ludbury House, so she lets us in. I glance around the mansion while she sets a doorstop in place by the wooden front door. It's an impressive space with a two-story foyer, a crystal chandelier, and a grand staircase. Antique furniture fits right in with the historic mansion. "This is the first time I've been inside here. So this is where all the weddings happen?"

"Yup, except Mom and Dad's wedding. They got married

at a castle on the island of Villroy at the invitation of the prince."

"What!"

"Long story. You can ask Mom about it next time you see her."

"You have a very interesting family."

She offers her hand to shake. "Thank you in advance."

I take her hand and hold it. "For what?"

"For the performance to come. Let's get the stuff."

Several minutes later, I carry the china cabinet to the dining room. We carry the buffet in together, maneuvering it into place.

She wipes her hands on her jeans. "Now we have to return the truck to my parents' house and stop in to give Mom all the details. I'll be lovey-dovey with you. Try to look happy about it."

I cock my head. "What exactly is lovey-dovey in front of your parents?"

"You'll see."

This should be interesting.

A short time later, we're standing on her parents' porch, Mackenzie's hand in mine as she uses her other hand to push the doorbell.

Her dad answers the door. "Hey, sounds like it went well." He doesn't comment on the hand-holding, but he does glance at our clasped hands, filing the info away.

He steps back, and I follow Mackenzie inside. Hailey waves from the recliner chair with her feet up.

"Thank you both!" Hailey says. "I so appreciate it. How does it look in the space?"

"Good!" Mackenzie says brightly. She puts her hand on my arm and gazes up at me. "Cal was wonderful. So helpful and strong."

I square my shoulders, pride filling me. Like Mackenzie actually adores me, even though I know it's just an act.

"Wonderful!" Hailey says.

I go to help Mackenzie off with her coat, but she shakes me off. "We're not staying."

"Oh, please stay," Hailey says. "I'd love to offer dinner as a thank you."

"I bought steaks," Josh says. "Plenty for the four of us."

My mouth waters. I love steak, and Josh is a great cook. I guess he'd have to be with his restaurant.

Mackenzie sends me a look that says, *See? I told you.* She's so sure about the matchmaking. It seems to me her mom genuinely wants to thank us for doing her a favor.

"I love steak," I say.

Mackenzie smiles at me tightly. I help her off with her coat. She takes it and hangs it in the hall closet and holds out her hand for mine. Josh heads into the kitchen, but Hailey's still parked in the recliner on account of her ankle. I can feel her watching us.

I guess Mackenzie does too because after she hangs my coat up, she puts a hand on my chest and smiles up at me. My heart kicks harder. "Great job," she whispers.

Hailey looks at us, her brows drawn together with concern. "Cal, would you mind going into the kitchen to see if we have any cabernet? Josh will know where it is."

"Sure."

Mackenzie sits on the sofa near her mom, sending me a flirty wave with a smile. I wave back, enthralled despite myself. I know it's fake, but damn if I don't like it.

9

Mackenzie

Mom's all concern as she studies my expression. "You seem closer to Cal after your outing today."

I lean into it. "He's a great guy. Strong, capable, smart."

Her hand goes to her throat, seeming taken aback. "Well, yes," she says slowly. "I can see why you'd think that, but let's not forget he's a bit of a player, isn't he? He was dumped on Valentine's Day for not proposing to his live-in love. I don't want to see you get hurt."

"You know me, Mom. I'll be careful."

"I know you say you'll be careful, but it's easy to misstep, and the next thing you know, it's a slippery slope to major heartache. I don't want that for you."

Then why do you keep throwing us together? I've committed to the fake-boyfriend scheme, so it's too late to let on that I'm onto her. Besides, direct confrontation got me nowhere last time.

"I'm a big girl," I say.

"You're a lady."

"Whatever."

She adjusts her leg on the recliner. "Okay. I've said my piece."

Cal returns with two glasses of red wine, handing one to Mom and one to me. I take a long drink.

Mom smiles sweetly. "Thank you, Cal. Please help yourself to something to drink. Josh has beer if you prefer that."

"I'm good." Cal sits next to me, widening his legs in typical manspreading, which makes it easy for me to shift ever so slightly so our knees are touching.

And then I put my hand on his knee in a bold gesture. Energy surges through my hand, a shock reminder of the chemical attraction. I dimly sense Mom's stare.

Cal takes my wandering hand and entwines our fingers together, like it's completely natural.

"Are you two officially a couple?" Mom asks. "I know people nowadays wait a while to say it's official."

"It's official," Cal says.

"It's complicated." Why did I say that? I'm supposed to be faking a relationship, not confessing the truth. That I'm all mixed up with inconvenient feelings and lust.

Cal stares at me. "It is?"

"So it's casual?" Mom asks, looking from me to Cal.

"Uh," he says.

"It's new," I say. "That's why it's complicated."

Mom nods. "Good communication goes a long way. If you understand expectations from the start, then there's no complications."

"Is that what you and Dad did," I ask pointedly, "before the war?" Their frenemy war is legend in town. It's hysterical.

Mom narrows her eyes.

"War?" Cal asks.

"I'll go see if your dad needs help." Mom lowers the recliner's footrest and attempts to get up with her ankle boot. Cal springs into action, helping her to her feet and handing her the crutches.

"Thank you," she says with great dignity before making her way to the kitchen.

Cal returns to my side, leaning close. "What war? Seems like a touchy subject."

"Oh, it is. I'll let her tell it, or you can ask Dad for an alternate-universe version."

He looks so adorably baffled with his brows crinkled like that. I smooth them out.

"What are you doing?" he whispers. I suppress a shiver as memories of his sexy whispers flood me.

"What we talked about." My voice sounds a little breathy. I attempt to put some distance between us, but I'm caught between the armrest of the sofa and Cal's body. Temptation has never been so strong.

God, I want him. He smells so good.

"What's with saying it's complicated?" he asks.

I shrug, my arm brushing against his. "I don't know. It just came out."

"So what do we call it?"

I face him, grab his shirt, and pull him close. "Complicated." We're so close I feel his sharp intake of breath. Slowly, his hand moves, cupping the back of my neck. A moment of shimmering tension hangs in the space between us before I close the distance, sinking into a kiss that feels as inevitable as breathing. My pulse jumps as his mouth slants over mine, taking control. Why did I give this up?

"Mom made bruschetta," Dad announces.

Cal and I jerk apart. Cal looks guilty. As for me, I'm thinking Cal and I aren't done.

Dad sets a plate of bruschetta on the coffee table in front of us, gives Cal a *touch my daughter and die* look, and checks in with me. Overprotective much? I smile.

"Thank you, sir," Cal says, taking a piece of bruschetta.

Dad grunts and turns back to the kitchen.

Cal

Dinner was amazing. Steak done perfectly, baked potatoes with crispy onions and cheese, and steamed broccoli. Josh marinated the meat for hours beforehand. It's like Mackenzie's parents knew we'd stay for dinner.

Mackenzie sits directly across from me at the table. I caught her sneaking looks at me while we ate, or maybe that was me sneaking looks at her.

"Would you like to stay for dessert?" Hailey asks. "We have ice cream from Shane's Scoops."

Mackenzie tilts her head. "Mmm, tempting, but Cal and I have plans after this."

Josh and Hailey exchange a look. It's like a secret conversation, though I'm not getting any negative vibes from it.

"Oh? What are your plans?" Hailey asks.

"Cal asked me to take a look at his new place for some decorating ideas," Mackenzie says.

"Decorating," Josh says. "Is that code for—" He jerks and abruptly goes silent. I think Hailey kicked him under the table with her good foot.

I don't blame him for calling Mackenzie on it. Like any guy would invite a woman to his place for the purpose of decorating on a Saturday night. Still, I back her up. "Just a question on the living room layout; then we're going to watch a movie. Mackenzie has never seen *Field of Dreams*, the best baseball movie of all time."

"I've seen *Bull Durham*," she says, like our earlier conversation in the car.

"That's a relationship movie."

She narrows her eyes. "It's definitely a baseball movie. Let's watch both."

"If we're going to have a doubleheader, I vote for *Moneyball*."

"We can discuss," she says airily.

Hailey smiles serenely. Even Josh seems okay with us.

Mackenzie gives me a lovesick smile, which sends chills down my spine because it's not real. My mind knows it's not real, but my body senses danger. My pulse rushes through my ears, all sounds fading to a dull roar.

Mackenzie stands abruptly. I do too. She puts her hand on my arm. "You're the guest so sit. I'll clear the dishes. I'll make you work later." She gives me a sexy smile, leaving me stunned in a good way, the panic receding.

I watch her go, hips swaying as she balances dishes expertly.

When I turn back, Hailey's smiling at me. A big smile, almost proud, like I'm the best guy she could imagine for her daughter. She turns to Josh, and he inclines his head.

Was that parental approval? I don't dare let Mackenzie in on the secret. She'd want to end our fake relationship before it even got started. And it seems really important to her.

A deception within a deception on the woman who started it all. Is that playing dirty? Maybe. But the alternative, not seeing her again, doesn't sit well with me either.

I'll take a wait and see approach. That's only sensible.

She pops back in and smiles at me. "Ready?"

I can't say no to this woman. That should scare me more than it does. "Ready."

Mackenzie

So here we are at Cal's apartment in Clover Park. He has the entire second floor of a house. It's cozier than I thought it'd be. Built-in bookcases flank a fireplace, and he actually has books in them. A man who reads, yum. There's a cushy navy sectional sofa. I imagine his bedroom is equally nice, but we won't be going in there tonight.

"Want anything?" he asks, taking my coat. He hangs it on a hook by the door.

"No, thanks." I'm suddenly almost shy. This feels kinda like a date—dinner and then a movie. Well, dinner with my parents and then a movie at home.

"I actually have it on DVD," he says, rummaging around in the drawer of a coffee table.

A few minutes later, he presses play on *Field of Dreams*.

"Hit the lights," he says.

Oh, we're going to sit in the dark together. Okay, no problem, standard movie procedure. I turn off the lights and join him on the sofa. Then I grab a throw pillow and hug it, mostly so I'm not tempted to climb into his lap and kiss him. I breathe in his scent, like soap and pure sexy man.

I glance sideways at him as he settles back, resting his feet on the coffee table. He seems to be into the movie. I should pay attention so I can argue more intelligently why *Bull Durham* is better.

Before long, I'm pulled into the movie, my throw pillow long forgotten. Oh my gosh, the players are all here in the field of dreams. They showed up! And his dad. My throat tightens, my eyes stinging with tears. When the end credits roll, I have to wipe the tears from my cheeks.

"Are you crying?" he asks.

I sniffle. "No."

"You are. See, I told you it was the best baseball movie of all time."

"No, that's still *Bull Durham*."

"I don't have that one. Let's watch *Moneyball*."

"If we're going to have a triple-header, I insist *Bull Durham* is next. Find it on a streaming service."

His lips twitch. "There's no such thing as a triple-header."

"All the more reason to watch *Bull Durham* next." I pull out my phone. "I'll look up where to watch it. You make the popcorn."

He stares at me, not moving to get snacks like a reasonable person. "You're willing to watch three baseball movies in a row? You must really be a fan of baseball."

"I'm a fan of good stories, and this is the only way to prove my movie is best."

He cocks his head. "You've never asked me about my baseball-playing days."

"Do you want to talk about it?"

"Not really, but most people are fans. They want to know."

"I've been to my brothers' games as a kid, and a few times I saw Yankees games in person. My favorite part was the snacks."

"Oh."

"Speaking of…" I smile encouragingly.

He tugs a lock of my hair. "Popcorn. How do you know I have popcorn?"

I grab the remote. "You have a cozy apartment. I figured you have the appropriate snacks." A sudden worry occurs. "You don't have the microwave kind, do you?"

"I have the already-made kind in a bag."

"Next time we'll do this at my place, and I'll make you fresh popped."

His brows lift. "You're assuming a lot."

I freeze. Omigod. I'm such an idiot. "I was just enjoying myself. Sorry to assume. We don't have to keep watching movies. It's late." I stand, trying to find my purse in the glow of the TV screen.

He grabs me by the wrist and tugs me back to the sofa. "Hey, speedy. I didn't say leave. You're just bossier than I'm used to."

I nearly say, *You're bossy in the bedroom. I'm bossy everywhere else*. Probably best not to bring sexy times up when we're in friend mode.

I play it cool. "Oh, well, I am the oldest of my siblings. I had to keep my brothers in line."

He lifts my hand and kisses the palm. Tingles race up my arm. "I like it."

"Then what're you teasing about? Go get the popcorn, man. And when you get back, set it up for the movie. I found it on several streamers."

Once we're all settled with popcorn and water, Cal starts the movie. I settle in with a handful of popcorn. This is fun.

An hour later, I pull the soft throw blanket from the back of the sofa and put it over us both. He slips an arm around my shoulders, and it feels natural to lean my head against his shoulder. The heat between us wraps around me, relaxing every muscle. Desire stirs, but I ignore it.

But then there's a sexy onscreen kiss, and I'm remembering our kiss. And another sexy scene and another. I don't dare look up at him.

The next thing I know, he's shifting off the sofa, leaving me behind under the blanket. I sit up. The movie's over. I blink, trying to get my bearings. "I must've dozed off."

"Good thing you've seen this relationship movie before."

I smile. "Baseball movie."

"We'll save *Moneyball* for next time. You can stay the night if you want."

I blink. Together in his bed, or I'm on the sofa while he sleeps in the bed? Either way the temptation is too great. No way am I putting myself through that. I used up all my willpower not kissing him during our movie marathon. "I'll go."

I pull off the blanket, stand, and fold it neatly, setting it back on the sofa.

He turns on the lights, dimming them. Then he gets my coat for me. He sure does a lot of polite sweet gestures considering no one is here to witness them for our fake dating.

He helps me on with my coat, and I find myself blushing over all the fuss. Obviously I don't need help, but it's like he wants to care for me. No guy has ever made this much effort.

I flip my hair out of the collar of my coat and turn to him. "Want to meet up for a run tomorrow morning? I figure it'll be a good public outing for our fake relationship."

"How do you know I run?"

"You don't get a body like that at home." I slap a hand over my mouth.

He grins. "My knee doesn't cooperate for a run, but I can join you on a walk. We'll get a lot of eyes on us on Main Street."

"That works. I'll text you in the morning. Thanks."

"You know, you can get this body at home," he says with a wink. "Just need the right training regimen."

I shake my head, thoroughly embarrassed. "Goodnight, Cal."

He leans in, and my heart thuds for a crazy moment. But then his kiss lands on my cheek. "Goodnight, Mackenzie."

I step out, smiling. Who knew I could have so much fun with a guy friend? Fake dating was a great idea.

10

I'm energized this morning despite my late movie night with Cal. I already texted him about meeting up soon. We're going to Something's Brewing Café for coffee. Nice high-visibility setting. I know we've already convinced Mom we're a couple, but we have to follow through being seen around town together for a while more. Keeping it realistic is very important.

I hand Harper a mug of coffee and join her at our kitchen table with a tall glass of water.

Harper sips her coffee and eyes me blearily over the rim. "So you actually went back to his place? How is that a public fake relationship?"

I give Felix a scritch behind his ear. He jumped on my lap as soon as I sat down. "Well, I had never seen his favorite movie of all time, and it sounded good. I even teared up at the end."

"And then he comforted you and took you to bed?"

I laugh even as heat rises to my cheeks. "No! Then I insisted he watch my favorite baseball movie." I fan myself. "I forgot how many seriously sexy scenes are in *Bull Durham*. It would've been awkward, but by that point we were cuddled up on the couch."

"Cuddled up? Mac—"

"In a platonic way."

"Does platonic mean foreplay in your world?"

"Just because you haven't had a guy friend since you and Nathan—"

"We were in second grade! Back then, a boy friend was the exact same thing as a girl friend but with more balls."

I snort. "The sport kind or the other kind?"

"Both!"

We crack up.

I pull a hairband from my pocket, putting my hair into a ponytail. "Well, we're all adults now. I'm sure Nathan would be happy to be your guy friend if you ever stopped hating on him long enough."

She sips her coffee, her expression shuttering closed. "No hate, just no love. There's a difference."

"I'm going on a run." I leave out that I'm running to meet up with Cal. She'll make a big deal out of it.

I stand and do a few stretches.

"Have fun on your freezing cold run."

I smile and wave. "I will."

I jog by Cal's new apartment and find him on the sidewalk, already waiting for me. His lips curve up slowly, like he's pleased to see me. "Morning."

Warmth fills my chest. "Morning."

He joins me, and we start walking toward Main Street. "So what's new since I last saw you?"

I laugh. "A lot's happened in those nine hours. Sleep, a shower, oh, I encouraged Harper to have a guy friend. Have you ever had a woman friend before me?"

His brows draw together. "I was too busy working in the city to meet a lot of women, but I've met a lot of women here. I guess they could become friends, but I don't really see the point."

I nearly break stride. I thought I was the only woman he'd

met. Is he hooking up with other women while we fake date? Because that would look bad.

He glances at me. "You okay? Do you want me to have more women friends?"

"No, forget I asked. Just making conversation."

"Looking forward to our next movie night. You did invite me over for fresh-popped popcorn."

I smile so big my cheeks hurt. He wants to come over. Does this mean something more than friends? I could be reading too much into it.

"I've got a nosy roommate," I say, waiting for him to say it doesn't matter. That would mean friends.

He says nothing. Hmm…

"Fair warning, we'll be watching my favorite movies," I say. "I feel like two baseball movies in a row is plenty."

"Okay, what movies?"

"*Wonder Woman* and *The Woman King*."

"So you're a fan of kickass female-lead movies."

I lift my brows. "Problem?"

"They turn me on too." He grins. I give him a playful shove, and he pulls me in for a quick squeeze before releasing me. He's charming, even first thing in the morning. But can we get back to all the other women he's met?

"My sister loves *Wonder Woman* too," he says.

What women has he met?

He keeps talking, oblivious to my increasing agitation. "I'm a fan of Claire's action movies too. Actually, I've seen all of her movies. You probably have too since she's your aunt, right?"

I stop short on the sidewalk. "You can't be with other women while we fake date."

He cocks his head. "So it's a monogamous fake relationship?"

I gesture around town, though no one's out yet. "It's hardly convincing if people see you running around town with other women."

He gives my ponytail a tug. "So you can't be running around town with other men either."

I lift my chin. "I'm not."

"I'm not either. You're the first woman to invite me on a fake-relationship walk."

"What other women have you met?" I blurt and instantly regret it.

His smile is wide. "You like me."

I pick up the pace, glad for the cold breeze. My cheeks are flaming hot.

He says, "I've met all your female family members and a few clients."

Beyond embarrassed, I mumble, "Doesn't matter."

After a long pause while I reconsider my life choices, he says, "What's our next public date in your planner? Should we have a shared online calendar?"

I get the nagging feeling he's teasing me about my fake-date plan. But how else can I catch Mom in the act and put an end to her crazy matchmaking once and for all?

Cal is the opposite of a sure thing. He has to earn my trust. Maybe after a platonic relationship for, oh, six months, then I'd *consider* a relationship.

Okay, I'm scared out of my mind. I've never felt this way before, sort of light and fizzy when we're talking and stupid with lust the rest of the time. A dangerous combo. My instincts tell me to run. But I can't let him know he's getting to me.

I pick up the pace to a fast walk.

"Is there a reason we're speedwalking?" he asks.

"I've got some energy."

"You're the first person I've met who gains energy as they walk in the winter."

"Spring is only twelve days away."

"You're counting the days?" He sounds amused. I wish I could feel as casual as he sounds.

"Let me check the town events calendar, and I'll get back to you."

"There's always Sunday family dinner tonight." He gives me an adorable lopsided smile. "I have an open invitation."

I stare at him. "Are you insane? We did family dinner last night."

"Will you be there?"

"I *have* to go. Save yourself."

"I like your family."

I shake my head even as part of me warms at the sentiment. "Let's stay focused." And then I promptly trip on a raised sidewalk square. "Aah!" I'm about to fall flat on my face when Cal wraps his arms around me, my back to his front.

My heart races purely from the adrenaline of nearly falling.

Miss Smith leans out her front door in her bathrobe and slippers. "Are you okay, Mackenzie?"

Cal loosens his hold but keeps his hands on my arms. He's putting on a show. I put my hand over his. "Yes, Miss Smith, thank you. My boyfriend caught me."

She squints. "Who's that?"

Cal waves. "Cal Davis. I'm the new town lawyer taking over for Gabe Reynolds."

Her lips pucker. "A lawyer." She shuts the door.

I turn to Cal. "That's good. Spotted already by Miss Smith as a couple." We continue on our way to Main Street.

"Is she a central part of the town gossip line?"

"Not really. She's a retired librarian hell-bent on keeping things quiet. Not easy in this town."

"So looks like we definitely need to be seen by more people. We should stay at Something's Brewing for a bit. Another fake date in the books."

"Mmm." I'm starting to feel a little silly, like maybe he thinks this is a weird thing, and he's humoring me. But then why go along with it?

When we get to Something's Brewing Café, Cal holds the door open for me. Cal's the first man to put me first. At least through the doorway, and in line. I feel a little like a queen.

I point to the glass display case of cream puffs. They're small, about golf ball size, with a light flaky crust and sweet cream. "The special only on Sundays."

His hands go to my waist as he whispers in my ear, "Do you want one?" My knees go weak. He's very good at public affection.

I glance over my shoulder, my breath coming faster at his warm expression. "Just one?"

When it's our turn to order, I say, "I'll take an espresso for here, please."

"Make that two and six cream puffs," Cal says. I'm glad Cal understands the cream-puff situation.

We sit at a table with our espressos and cream puffs. I finish off one and hum my pleasure. Heaven.

Cal watches me intently.

"Try one," I say.

He takes one, pops it in his mouth whole, and gestures for me to have more.

I do. "Mmm." I so rarely treat myself to these, but they are to die for.

He leans forward, swiping his thumb across my upper lip. "Cream," he says before placing his finger in his mouth to taste. My insides tighten, a delicious ache lingering.

"Have another," he says in a sexy low tone.

Are we still talking about cream puffs? I'd rather not embarrass myself by leaping across the table and throwing myself at him.

"Uh, no, thank you," I say demurely.

I sip my espresso.

His eyes clash with mine, and the tension skyrockets between us. I want him. Badly. He wants me. I lick my lips, about to throw caution to the wind when Aunt Mad stops by the table.

Screech! That's my lust hitting the brakes. She's Dad's younger sister, a brash badass who raised four rambunctious boys while building an impressive real estate career. She's also Mom's best friend.

Aunt Mad's dressed casually in a flannel with jeans, her brown hair in a short bob. "Hey, Mackenzie, Cal. I'm heading next door to grab the book for our next book club meeting. You want in? Still time to read it. Meeting's a week from Thursday." She's entirely sincere.

"What're you reading?" Cal asks.

"It's a romance book club," I tell him. "The Happy Endings Book Club." Mom and friends love to swoon over mushy romance. Total fantasy. I'm much too practical to find the stories realistic.

One corner of his mouth tilts up. "What kind of happy ending?"

"The best kind," Aunt Mad says with a knowing smile.

Cal looks intrigued.

"No, thanks," I say quickly. "We have plans."

"Plans, huh?" Mad eyes the cream puff, points to Cal expectantly, and he gestures for her to take it. She pops the cream puff in her mouth, squeezes my shoulder, and heads out with her to-go coffee.

"That was good," I whisper to Cal. "She'll report back to Mom about our ongoing relationship. Now we don't need to plan something for today."

Cal looks over at the adjoining door to the bookstore. The café and Book It are owned by the same couple, Shane and Rachel O'Hare. "We should stop by their book club."

"And get caught in a two-hour discussion of a romance novel we haven't read?"

"There's still time!" He grins. "At least we could show off our lovey-dovey skills with witnesses."

I giggle. "It sounds silly when you say it."

This man is all in with my plan. I like him too much.

"Cal."

His dark eyes meet mine. "Mackenzie."

I'm dying to stroke his short beard, so I do. He grabs my hand and kisses my palm, sending a rush of heat through my arm. "Thank you."

"My pleasure."

The words vibrate through me, bringing every nerve to attention. Too intense for a fake relationship. I can't let this get out of hand.

I push back from the table. "I have a lot to do today, so I'm going to get back."

"Right. Me too."

I stand and put on my coat before he can help me with it. I'm getting caught up in this game, enjoying it too much. "Actually, I think I'm going to run for a bit, burn off some of these calories. I'll be in touch, okay?"

"What's wrong?"

I shake my head. "Nothing. Really. See ya!" I'm about to bolt when he grabs my arm. I look up at him.

"Mackenzie, what's wrong?"

I try to smile but can't manage it. How can I tell him I'm starting to fall for my own little game? He's too good at it, making me believe he really cares for me. All these nice gestures, his sexy sweetness. He even looked like he was considering reading a romance. I don't even read them. Do you know how many men read romance? One point three percent. I'm making that up, but it's unusual, and I know he's just being nice to Aunt Mad. Oh God. I have to get out of here!

"I missed my morning run," I blurt. "Need the endorphins."

"Sure?"

"Mmm-hmm." I try not to bolt.

"Okay. See you for our next fake date."

"Right. See ya." I move as quickly as I dare without looking like I'm fleeing the scene. I'm not sure I can handle another fake date.

I fully own that I freaked out. I can't handle seeing Cal so many times in a row without getting in too deep, so I didn't plan another fake date for this weekend. I saw him last weekend twice, so that's going to have to carry us for a couple of weeks. I need to slow this crazy ride down.

Instead I organized a girls' night with my besties at a club in NYC to enjoy the singles scene. Fake dating by definition means that we're both single. And I really need the change of scenery.

When the moment finally arrives, Harper and I are dressed to kill, hair and face on point. Harper's wearing an off-the-shoulder red dress that ends mid-thigh with killer white boots. I'm in a classic little black dress with my metallic-red spiked heels. These heels scream fun.

We wait in line to be let into the club. Our names are on the list thanks to our friend Shayla. She's filming a limited series in the city, and where she goes, her assistant, Olivia, goes. The four of us used to live together in the house where Harper and I live now. It was so much fun, except for the whole Shayla stalker situation. Long story, thankfully resolved.

We get the go-ahead from the bouncer and step past the velvet rope and inside. The thumping club music vibrates my eardrums. Harper grins at me, immediately pulling me through the crowded dance floor to the center of the action. Harper doesn't need a drink to let loose.

"Now this is what I'm talking about!" she shouts over the music. "Much better than the Valentine's dance, amiright?"

I nod even as Cal's face flashes in my mind from the Valentine's dance, those soulful eyes, our slow dance. The delicious heat. What's he doing on a Saturday night?

I really need to stop thinking about Cal. I watch as Harper dances freely, arms in the air as she checks out the guys dancing nearby. That's what I should be doing. I do my best to copy her, and eventually, I get into the music, dancing my heart out. Cardio is the best for emptying the mind.

Look at me enjoying the singles scene in the city that never sleeps!

Is it late? It feels late.

I lean close to Harper's ear. "When's Shayla getting here?"

Shayla has a private room booked for us upstairs, but Harper doesn't want to go there until after we meet some potential guys to bring with us. Of course I agreed because we're both single, and there's no reason not to meet guys.

Cal's husky voice runs through my mind. *Do you like this, Mackenzie?*

No more Cal.

"When she gets here," Harper says. "She's bringing some friends. Hope it's that hot guy from her new show."

"Which one?"

"Right? There's several potentials."

"He won't be sticking around if he's only here to film something."

Harper shrugs. See, there's the Harper I know and love. I don't know what all that tall, dark, and handsome stuff was before. Though she's still watching those old black-and-white romantic comedies. I've watched a few too, only because they were on.

"Hey," a masculine voice says behind me, making me jump.

I turn to find identical twin guys in their twenties—dark hair, one with scruff, the other clean-shaven, both handsome. *Nope*. Hints of our identical twin dads going on here.

Harper's reaction is the same. She shoos them away. "Wrong."

They look confused.

"Sorry," I say to them, "her dad's an identical twin, and she's got daddy issues."

The clean-shaven guy frowns. The scruffy one turns to me. "How about you?"

I consider. I'm not attracted to him, and now I can legit claim I'm enjoying the singles scene. Sounds like a go. "I'll dance with you."

He moves in close. "I'm Craig."

I shift back. "Mackenzie."

His twin calls, "Getting a drink!" before walking off the dance floor.

"What do you do?" Craig asks over the music. He's not a bad dancer.

"High-tech security."

"Cool. I'm in finance, but I'm not a finance bro. Ha-ha-ha!"

I'm about to say we don't have to talk when he launches into a detailed description of his job, yelling to be heard over the music. I dance, keeping Harper in the corner of my eye. She's dancing with a muscular guy wearing a light blue shirt unbuttoned to his navel. Six-pack abs, golden skin, slicked-back dark hair. He gets in close behind her. She turns, and they undulate body to body. Foreplay on the dance floor.

I face front. Craig finally stopped talking. I hope Shayla and friends get here soon.

"Can I get you a drink?" Craig asks, leaning in close.

"No, thanks."

He touches my arm, and I want to recoil. "Want to go someplace quieter to talk?"

I shake my head. Harper's arms are around her guy's neck, his leg between hers. My mind flashes to Cal's hands on my waist at the dance, firm and warm. And then night after night of big, competent hands roaming freely, learning my body, targeting all the right places.

"Excuse me," I tell Craig. "Need to make a call. Nice to meet you."

Craig frowns and works his way over to another woman. Guess he got the hint. I should've been interested in him. He seemed nice. Why am I at a club if not to meet someone new?

I skirt to the edge of the dance floor, keeping an eye on Harper. I check my phone. No texts from any guys I might know.

This is going to be a long night.

11

Cal

I've got to get Mackenzie out of my head. Visions of her long hair fanned out on my pillow, the smile that makes her blue eyes shine like she has a happy secret. For a while I thought I was her happy secret. Nope. Now she wants to fake date, and then she doesn't even set up a fake date for this weekend.

Is she expecting me to set up a fake date? I don't even know what qualifies. So here I am on a Saturday night in the city with some of my old coworkers, grabbing a beer at an Irish pub we used to meet at regularly. Conversation circles around who will make partner next. This is partly why I left. The insane competition and hours and for what? To work even more hours and then collapse from exhaustion, a heart attack, or worse.

Things changed for me at work when a partner in my firm got a late-stage cancer diagnosis. He regretted missing so much in life, always chained to his desk. That combined with memories of Mom's own cancer struggle put me on a different path. A better path.

"How's small-town life treating you, Cal?" Jack asks.

"Good," I say. "I like being my own boss. Better work-life balance."

"Yeah, but what a pay cut," Jack says with a bark of a laugh.

The group, two men and two women, all nod and give each other looks. I'm sure they've all discussed me and concluded I'm crazy for giving up big money for what they see as a small life.

"It's been really good so far," I say, smiling as I think of Mackenzie. But then I remember the way she bolted the last time I saw her, and basically disappeared from my life. What went wrong?

Jack claps me on the back. "Good for you." He sounds insincere.

"Happy for you," Sara says, sounding equally insincere.

I set my beer on the bar. "Gotta run. Good to see you all."

This elicits a round of "Aww!" "It's early!" "Stay!"

I smile. "Got to meet up with Rayna. The final splitting of our stuff."

"Oof! Don't be a stranger," Jack says.

I nod, but he's already turned back to the group. Conversation resumes quickly. I throw some bills on the bar and head for the door. The moment I step outside, I feel like I can breathe again. I don't miss the cramped bar scene. Not like Happy Endings where you get some elbow room.

Guess I'm not much of a city person anymore. Only took a month in Clover Park to make the city lose its shine.

A few minutes later, I've got a ride to my old apartment building. Rayna took over my lease with a new roommate, which was fine by me. When she texted asking me to stop by and pick up some stuff of mine, I was tempted to tell her to toss it, but since I was going to be in the city anyway, I agreed.

I'll just go in, grab my box of stuff, load up my car in the parking garage, and head back home. Clover Park is home now. In no small part due to Mackenzie. What is going on with us? It's complicated like she said before. I'm confused and disappointed. I was starting to get into the fake-dating scheme.

It's not like I want something serious. Not anymore.

Learned my lesson. Relationships and I don't get along. And I can't forget that Hailey warned Mackenzie away from me. I owe Hailey a lot. Not only did she introduce me around town, but she continues to invite me to local events that could help me make even more connections. Her reach is wide, and her rep is gold.

Enough about Mackenzie and the entire Campbell family. I can't believe how much headspace she takes up. Somehow my work-life balance has tipped into hardly ever focusing on work and exclusively thinking of one person.

I shake it off and press the intercom buzzer to get into my old apartment building. The door unlocks, and I head upstairs.

When I walk into the apartment, I find Rayna and a guy I've never seen before sitting on the couch. He's got a mane of messy curly blond hair, a ripped T-shirt, jogging pants, and bare feet. Is this the roommate?

Rayna leaps up. "Hi, Cal."

"Hi."

"This isn't what it looks like," she says, gesturing behind her. "He's paying to stay on the couch. My roommate's out with her friends."

"None of my business," I say, surprised how little it bothers me. I used to get worked up every time she met up with her ex for drinks or dinner or some rally. She can be with any guy she wants now. I'm over it.

Blondie sits up and puts an arm around her. "I'm not just a couch surfer. I'm her guy."

"He's not." She turns to him. "Couch surfing is over. Go now, please."

He grabs his coat and backpack from a nearby chair and slips on his sandals by the door. "This is messed up."

Rayna shuts the door behind him and locks it.

I exhale sharply. She knew I was coming over and waited until I got here to tell him to leave. She wants me to be jealous. It occurs to me she wanted me to be jealous of her ex, too, not just shove his superior emotional availability in my face like she always said. Either way, I was jealous that she was out with him so much, but now, well, if Rayna wants to hook up with random couch surfers, it's none of my business. I haven't exactly been lonely since our breakup.

"My stuff?" I ask.

"In the bedroom." She gestures for me to follow. "It's heavy. I found a lot of your books mixed in with mine and some other things."

Rayna stops next to the bed, folding her hands together in front of her. "Cal, I'm sorry about the way things ended. I shouldn't have thrown your law books at you."

I freeze, surprised by her apology. I was just as much to blame for letting things go on so long when I was unhappy. "It's okay. I'm sorry things ended so badly between us."

She nods, her brown eyes shiny with tears. "I wish I could take it all back. It was my own expectations that made me upset. We never talked about marriage. I can wait as long as you need. Cal, I still love you."

"I think you had the right idea," I say as gently as I can manage. "We weren't meant to be for the long haul, and you were the one brave enough to face it."

"I was wrong."

"No, you weren't. It's better that we both move on." I clear my throat, about to attempt amends in foreign emotional territory. "I, uh, should've been more honest with you about the way I was feeling after you moved in. I was in over my head. We were in different places, and I'm sorry for any hurt I caused you."

She crumples into tears and leans into my shoulder. I hold her, feeling bad about her tears while at the same time wanting to leave. This was our relationship in a nutshell.

After a few minutes, Rayna lifts her head and tries to kiss me. I shift away in time.

She wipes her eyes. "It's really over?"

"Yes."

She sniffles. "Your stuff is in the closet." She leaves, shutting the door behind her.

I go to the closet and pull out a box with several books, along with mementos she must've saved from our relationship. A dried rose, a cocktail napkin, concert ticket stubs, a birthday card, and my old jersey. I'm glad to get my jersey back. She liked to sleep in it. I don't have the equivalent box of relationship stuff to give her. I guess I wasn't sentimental about our time together. Is this what she meant when she complained I was closed off, or was it that I never liked to talk about deep emotional stuff? How can you talk about something you no longer feel?

When I step out of the room with my box, she says, "Cal, I thought you should know my therapist says you need therapy. If you never open your heart, you'll never be happy."

"How's that working out for you?"

Her face crumples. I take a step toward her, instantly regretting the words, and she holds up her palms. Dammit. I always end up saying the wrong thing when someone gets emotional.

"Rayna, I'm sorry. I'm not cut out for relationships. I hope you find a man you deserve. Not that couch-surfer guy. Someone who appreciates you."

She throws her hands in the air. "You say things like that right after stomping on my feelings, showing a glimmer of boyfriend potential. This is why you drive me crazy!"

"Okay."

She goes into the bedroom and slams the door.

I let out a breath of relief and walk toward the front door. The bedroom door opens again, and she yells, "I hope you're happy in your new place because I'm very happy!"

I'm not unhappy. But I don't say that. I don't say anything at all. Her ever-changing moods aren't my problem anymore.

Mackenzie

An eternity and two mojitos later, I'm bouncing along in

time to the music when Harper grabs my arm. "Come on, Shayla's here."

I follow her upstairs, as does the muscular guy barely wearing a shirt she latched onto, Felipe. Girls' night plus one. Honestly, I wasn't exactly eager to meet someone new. It's better this way. Focus on work. I'm not even sure I want to fake date anymore. Men are exhausting.

The private upstairs space has a sleek vibe with leather sofas and chairs, cool sconces, its own bar, and a view of the dance floor. I immediately spot Shayla's beaming smile as she approaches. Her long blonde hair is dyed red for her new role. It suits her. Two hulking bodyguards stand a short distance away.

Oh, look! She brought some unexpected guests sitting at a table in the back—my business partners, Owen and Nathan. Otherwise known as Shayla's husband/Harper's big brother (Owen) and Harper's sworn enemy (Nathan). Our old roommate Olivia's here too!

"Shayla!" I throw my arms around her. "It's been too long."

"I know, I know!"

I pull back to smile at her. "Working nonstop. I forgive you."

Olivia, a no-nonsense brunette, approaches wearing a loose navy dress with her signature black steel-toed boots. She's Shayla's assistant for now. She went to film school and has big goals. I swear she'll run Hollywood one day. "How's it going?" Olivia says. "Keeping busy?"

I give her a hug. "Yes. Not as busy as you, I'm sure."

Shayla throws an arm around Olivia's shoulders. "Olivia's helping me start my own production company. She's going to be my producer."

I smile. "Wow. Congrats to you both."

Harper walks over from the back table, her expression tight. Felipe waits a short distance away. "Shay, what are Owen and Nathan doing here on our girls' night?"

"You brought a guy up here," I say to Harper.

She ignores me in favor of staring down Shayla.

"Hello to you, too," Shayla says, hugging her.

"Sorry, it's just—"

"Owen doesn't count," Shay says, like husbands are background. That could be the case since Owen's entire attention tends to stay on Shay, but he's also Harper's brother, which means she can't hang with her new muscled guy without some annoying big-brother interference. "And Nathan was in the city for some kind of finance meeting, so Owen brought him along."

My brows scrunch together in confusion. "A finance meeting on a Saturday?"

Shay waves airily. "One of those networking things. I'm sure he'll fill you in."

Harper turns to Olivia. "Sorry, I was distracted. Great to see you! Love your purse. The beads on the burlap really pop. Did you make it yourself?" Before Olivia can respond, Felipe joins us and takes a picture of Shayla.

"Can I get a selfie?" he asks.

"No," Shayla says, glancing back at her bodyguards. It's beyond rude. He didn't even wait for an introduction before taking her picture.

One of Shayla's bodyguards comes over. "No unauthorized photos. Delete it. Now." He watches as Felipe deletes the picture. "Now delete it from the recently deleted folder." Felipe scowls but follows orders.

Harper turns on Felipe. "I told you to be chill. If you can't do that, leave."

Felipe frowns. "I'm chill. I just wanted a selfie. Guess the great Shayla Adler doesn't care about the little people."

"Bye, Felipe," Harper says, signaling to the guard.

Felipe lifts his palms and leaves.

"Sorry you had to ditch him because of me," Shayla says.

Harper shakes her head. "I'm here for a girls' night." She glances to the back table, where Owen and Nathan are sitting, and turns back, her lips set in a flat line. "Talk about a cock block," she says under her breath.

"More like a vag block," Olivia supplies helpfully. "Or a clam jam if you want to continue the rhyme scheme."

We all stare at her.

"What?" Olivia asks. "I don't believe in using male termi-nology for women. It's an erasure of our uniqueness."

"Relax," Shay says. "They're not going to get in the way of our fun." She waves at them. Owen stands and bumps Nathan's arm to stand too. They walk over.

Owen pulls Shay close and kisses the top of her head. "Hey, all. Hope you don't mind us crashing."

"Not at all," I say. "Any news from your networking?" I ask Nathan.

He tears his gaze from Harper, who's suddenly very inter-ested in imaginary lint on her dress. "I met up with a friend of a friend for a drink. This Wall Street guy. I'll send you the details if it goes anywhere."

"Cool," I say. "It'd be great to have a real foothold with the finance sector."

"Nathan's thinking of selling his house," Owen says. Nathan lives in Eastman, the town next to Clover Park.

Harper's head snaps up. "Really?"

Nathan searches her expression. "Thinking about it. I could network a lot more with finance decisionmakers if I move to the city."

"And for a woman," Owen says.

Harper stiffens, stealing a sideways glance at Nathan.

Nathan shakes his head. "It's like the bro code means nothing to you."

Owen grins. "Couldn't resist."

"Our champagne's here!" Shayla says. "Let's sit over there and have a toast."

Two waiters bring the champagne and glasses to a large round table with plush leather seats.

As we walk over, Harper whispers in my ear, "What woman?"

"No idea," I say. Nathan's never been serious about anyone.

After everyone has a glass, Shayla lifts hers in a toast. "To new ventures!"

We all toast to that.

"And friends!" I say, lifting a glass. We toast again.

"Does anyone want to dance?" Shayla asks. "I don't mind if you want to go downstairs for a bit. I've got Owen to keep me company here."

"I'll go if you ladies want to go," Nathan says.

"Mackenzie and I've already been down there," Harper says.

"She met Felipe," I say.

Nathan's brows lift. "The guy with the wardrobe malfunction?" He gestures to the buttons on his shirt respectfully buttoned up.

"It was sexy," Harper says. "Never mind. He sucks."

"How about you?" Nathan asks Olivia.

"Me?" Olivia squeaks. "No, thanks. I'm not looking for a man. Not that you were asking me out. I, uh, no, thanks." Bright pink splotches bloom on her cheeks and neck.

"When was the last time you hooked up with a sexy guy?" Harper teases Olivia.

I elbow Harper in the ribs. "Maybe she isn't looking for a guy. It's cool either way, Olivia."

Olivia rolls her eyes. "I'm just busy with work. After I'm better established, I'll think about a relationship *with a man*."

"So my little brother has a chance?" I ask.

"Finn and I are pen pals," Olivia says.

"Do you frame his poems?" I ask.

She crosses her arms. "He's sending me poems for my opinion, that's all. He's trying to get published."

I knew he was sending her poems! I bet she helps him with the rhyme scheme. Clam jam was genius. Ha!

"And all I want is a text," Harper says on a sigh.

"You can't even get a text?" Nathan asks. "What kind of guys are you—"

"What's her name?" Harper asks.

Nathan's brows scrunch in confusion. "Whose name?"

Shayla waves excitedly in the distance. "Claire! You made it!" Claire is Claire Jordan, Harper's mom, famous actor, director, and producer. Hollywood royalty. Well, so is Shayla. They're just like us only prettier, richer, and well-traveled. Ha! You couldn't pay me to live in the spotlight. I like my privacy.

Harper stares with dismay as her mom approaches. "Why does Shayla hate me?"

Aunt Claire hugs Shayla. They pull back, hands on each other's arms as they talk animatedly.

"She's not like a regular mom," Olivia says to Harper. "She's cool. She's Claire Jordan."

Harper sends Olivia a dark look. "And my personal clam jam."

Olivia fights a smile, probably pleased her suggested phrasing caught on.

I'd like to judge Harper for not being chill about hanging with her very cool mom, but I know if my mom were here, it would officially kill the vibe. I can't be next to Mom without the comparisons. I can never measure up to the beauty queen. That's a fact.

Mom never stopped trying to instill the importance of being a classy lady into me. Sometimes I think she's a throwback to the 1920s. For real. Dad says she used to insult him by calling him a cad. I had to look it up—a man who disregards others' feelings. It really was a word thrown around in those black-and-white movies she loves. Turns out she's a fan. So is Harper now. Are they meeting behind my back? They both have delusions of romance. I prefer comedies for my escape from reality.

"Family reunion at the club!" I crack up because it's not my mom and brother.

Harper sends me a murderous look before throwing me under the bus as soon as Aunt Claire joins us. "Mackenzie's seeing someone."

"Shut. Up." She knows about the fake dating, but she also knows I haven't followed up with it because I'm not sure I can handle being so close to him without being close to him, and I mean that in every sense of the word—physically and emotionally.

Anyway, Aunt Claire will blab to Mom, and then I'll have to pretend I'm into him some more when I'm trying so hard not to be into him, and I can't even blame Mom for this mess because she told me to keep my distance from the beginning.

"Ooh," Aunt Claire says. "Who is it?"

"No one," I say.

Harper continues, "Remember Cal, the baseball player slash lawyer from the Valentine's Day dance?"

My cheeks heat. "It's nothing. Nathan, you should get in touch with my aunt Mad to sell your house."

"Sure," Nathan says. "It's not definite yet."

"Go, Mackenzie," Shayla says. "A ball player. What team?"

"Some minor league team," I mumble.

"Triple A Iowa Cubs," Nathan says.

"Right, I forgot." I search desperately for another topic of conversation. "So what's the name of your new production company, Shay?"

"They didn't do much talking at all," Harper says.

"I remember him," Aunt Claire says. "He's gorgeous. Broad shoulders—"

"Can we not talk about this?" I say at the same time as Harper says, "Mo-om!"

"What? I notice things," Aunt Claire says.

"You should've invited him tonight!" Shayla says. "Let's text him now."

"Yeah, let's," Harper says.

"It's girls' night," I say. "Another time." I turn to Shayla. "Tell us all about your new production company. Do you have a name?"

"That's what I wanted to talk to you guys about," Shayla says. "I want to name it in honor of you, Claire, a play off of your Red Jewel Films." That's Claire's production company. "Something like Ruby Sisters Productions. Olivia will be my partner on it, and she's become like a sister."

Olivia bites her lower lip, her eyes watering. Wow, I've never seen her emotional before.

Aunt Claire puts a hand over her heart. "Oh, sweetheart, I'm honored and so proud of you!"

They launch into excited business talk, where they mostly rave about each other's artistic vision. Olivia chimes in with her practical business advice.

Harper wanders over to the rail, looking down at the dance floor. Nathan joins her. She glances at him, but he says nothing. Just keeping her company. They were childhood best friends. He even took her to the prom. I could never get her to say what exactly her issue is with him.

I pull my phone from my purse and do a quick Google search on Cal Davis purely out of curiosity. My stomach drops. A lot of images here of Cal with beautiful women at galas, games, restaurants, outside the Harvard club.

A bit more digging, and I see he played ball for a college team down South before the minors. After baseball, he went to Harvard law. I guess we never really took the time to get to know each other that well. Mostly surface fun stuff. But that's what I wanted, right?

I wonder which one of these beautiful women lived with him. I can only imagine how I compare to these glamourous women. I'm more the girl-next-door type. Obviously he's not going to go out of his way to fake date me or real date me. He's got his pick!

"Earth to Mackenzie!" Shayla waves her hand in front of my face.

"Huh?"

"This is Rick and Max, my costars." I look up at two guys standing next to Shayla. One tall and thin, the other average size but jacked with muscle. Neither one compares to Cal. Not that it matters.

Max offers his hand and gives me a firm handshake. "Mackenzie, nice to meet you. I'm Max Urban from *Blaze*. You might know me from *Seeker* too."

Barf. Next he'll bring up his IMDb page on his phone,

showing off all his TV and movie credits. To say I'm not impressed by Hollywood types is an understatement. I grew up in Claire Jordan's orbit. It's not as glamorous as it looks from the outside.

"Rick," the other guy says. "This is my first gig."

"Cool. Nice to meet you both."

Harper and Nathan join us, greeting the new guys. "I know you," Harper says to Max. "I loved you in *Seeker*."

His chest puffs out. "Want to get a drink?"

"Let's dance!" She grabs my arm. "Rick, join us."

"Anyone else want to join us?" I ask.

Nathan watches Harper, whose eyes are glued to Max and whatever he's bragging about. "No, thanks. Have fun."

I grab Olivia. "Come on, lady. Work break!"

"I like working," she grumbles, but she still follows me.

"Yay, Olivia!" Shayla cheers.

We go downstairs, and Rick pulls me into the throng of writhing bodies, immediately dancing too close. Where's Harper? Too many tall people block my view.

Rick puts his hand on my waist, shifting close. I shift back, out of reach, and turn toward Olivia, who's dancing in a strange box step, her eyes firmly upstairs, where Claire and Nathan watch us from above.

A couple of dances in, I'm tired of evading Rick's hands. I find Harper again and speak close to her ear. "I'm going home. Can you get a ride back with Owen?"

"It's early!"

"I'm done."

"Oh, fine."

"Keep an eye on Olivia."

We both glance over to where Olivia does a slow gyration, her hands swirling in the air. She almost looks like a genie coming out of her bottle. So cute.

I weave my way through the club, desperate for fresh air. Finally, I'm out the door. I take a refreshing breath of the cold night air. Just then I notice a man carrying a box crossing the street. My heart leaps to my throat.

Cal.

I practically run, so happy to see him that I bounce a little when I land in front of him on the sidewalk. "Hi! What're you doing here?"

"Mackenzie! This is a surprise. What're you doing here?"

I laugh. "I was at a club with my friends, but it got old. And you?"

"I was getting my last box of stuff from my ex."

I go on tiptoe and peek in the box because I'm nosy like that. "Bummer."

"It's all good. You want a ride back?"

"Sure!"

Cal

Once we clear the city limits, I finally address the elephant in the car. Not Mackenzie, ha-ha. "Are we done fake dating? I thought I'd hear from you to set up something this weekend."

"I'm sorry, I got busy with work, and then I had plans with friends."

"No problem." What now? I don't dare ask. Things are good again. She seemed so happy to see me. "How's this for a fake date—shopping on Main Street."

She smiles. "You really want to go shopping?"

"No, but I thought you'd like it."

"What do you like to do?"

"Watch hockey, play basketball, read. You like any of those things?"

"I read, but isn't that more of a solitary sport? Unless you want to read side by side in the library and hope someone gossipy wanders by."

"Is that a no on hockey and basketball?"

"No on hockey. I could play basketball, but your height advantage feels very unfair."

"I'll lift you for the slam dunk every time you steal the ball. That's what I used to do for my sister when she was little."

"Do you see me like a sister?"

I get serious. "No. Not at all."

"Cal, how is it that you bounced back so quickly from your ex? I imagine it must be hard to live with someone and then leave. Even tonight you got a box that basically says *It's over* in bold print, and you're here having fun with me."

"I always have fun with you."

She's quiet, not pushing me but giving me space to share about Rayna if I want to. Without pressure, it's easier for me to open up. "I guess, uh, Rayna felt I was too closed off, so she, uh, started seeing her ex, and that was hard for me."

"Of course it was hard for you. So she was living with you and cheating on you with her ex at the same time?"

"He had a girlfriend. She said they never crossed the line, more like they were best friends again. She said she could get her emotional needs met with him and her physical with me."

"Oh, Cal. That's not right."

"Yeah, so turns out the physical part fizzled out from the strain, and by the end we were more like roommates."

I turn off the highway, deflated from the unhappy memories. This is why I keep deep emotions locked away. They mess you up.

"Why did she think you'd propose on Valentine's Day, then?" she asks.

I force a flat neutral tone. "Because her ex got engaged, so she badly wanted us to get engaged too. Not because of me, because she was upset about him."

"I hate her."

I bark out a laugh. "It's fine."

"No, it is not fine. You didn't deserve that." She squeezes my arm. "Really, Cal. That's not how you deserve to be treated. You're a good man."

A lump of emotion lodges in my throat, preventing speech. I nod once.

We drive for a while in comfortable silence. When I glance over at her, she's sound asleep. I let out a slow breath, still overwhelmed by her kindness.

"You're the best person I've ever met," I whisper, only because I know she won't hear a word.

Mackenzie

I wake as the car slows for the turn down my street. Cal thinks I'm the best person he's ever met. I hold the sweet sentiment close to my heart. He whispered it when he thought I was sound asleep, so I don't want to bring it up. I want to hug him. I missed him and was so happy to run into him tonight. I've got a good man on my hands who makes me feel good, even though he comes with a lot of emotional baggage.

I've been cautious because he's on the rebound, but Rowan and Cooper were a rebound situation with her being left at the altar and then boom! She fell for Cooper, and now they're very happy together.

Look at me flipflopping about Cal when I'm normally on point with everything else in my life. But I don't want the night to end. I ache to touch him and feel his hands on me, to lose myself in the pleasure that is Cal.

He parks in front of my house. All the reasons for keeping my distance vanish the moment his eyes meet mine.

"Good, you're awake," he says. "I thought I'd have to carry you in."

Yes, please.

I'm the best person he's ever met. That must mean this is more than sex to him. It's time to take a risk.

"Will you?" I ask. "My roommate won't be home for hours."

He stares at me for a moment like he's considering the invitation.

"Please," I add softly.

He leans closer, pushing a lock of hair behind my ear. "Are you sure?"

I cup his face with both hands and kiss him. He returns

the kiss hungrily, his fingers wrapping around my hair as passion takes over, leaving us straining to get closer in the confines of the car. Raw need twists desperately inside me, urging me to take everything he gives.

He pulls away abruptly, breathing hard as his gaze smolders into mine.

I give him a sexy smile, feeling hopeful.

He gets out of the car, walks around, and opens the door for me. I hope this means he's coming in with me and not just walking me to the door.

I step out to find him searching my expression. "I want you, Cal."

He groans and scoops me up, cradled in his strong arms as he carries me to the front door. So romantic! Kind of like the groom carrying the bride over the threshold. *No, no, no, don't go there.*

"Let me down so I can open the door," I say.

He sets me down, his hands running up and down my sides as I fumble to get the key out of my purse. I push one of his hands away. He wraps the other arm around my waist, pressing me back against him, his voice a husky whisper in my ear. "I want you so bad. Can you feel how much I want you?"

His heat and hardness press into my backside, bringing a rush of desire that leaves my legs weak.

"Yes," I manage. "Don't touch me for a moment so I can get us in."

He chuckles and releases me.

I finally manage to get the door open, shut it, and lock it behind us. Then I grab his hand, leading him upstairs, turning on lights as I go.

Once in my room, I turn on the bedside lamp and face him, stripping out of my dress. He sucks in air as he takes me in wearing only panties, a strapless bra, and heels. The moment I step out of my heels, he wraps his arms around me.

"Let me do the rest." His voice is gravelly, scraping against my insides. He kisses along the column of my neck as he removes the bra, shifting to kiss and lick my breast before drawing my nipple into his mouth with a hard suck. I moan, my head dropping back.

He gives the other breast the same treatment, the tug of pleasure a direct line to my sex. His hands slide down my sides, slipping under the edges of my panties and peeling them down.

"God, Mackenzie, you're so sexy."

He makes me feel sexy. "Thank you. Your turn."

"Not yet. Lie on your back and spread your legs for me."

I comply, used to his commands in the bedroom. He directs the action, and my surrender is the ultimate pleasure for both of us.

He settles between my legs, shifting down to give me one long lick. My breath shudders out. He places my leg over his shoulder and then the other, leaving me wide open to his touch. A long moment passes where he just gazes at me. I whimper, dying for his touch.

"Cal, please, I need you so much."

"Good, baby, that's what I like to hear." He strokes with his fingers, delicately parting my folds before his tongue joins the action. My hips jerk. He hums against me, the vibrations rocking me to my core.

And then he slides a finger inside me as he works magic with his mouth. I rock helplessly against him, racing to the peak that's just out of reach. His name is a litany on my lips until no sound is possible. My fingers clutch the sheets as he takes me on a never-ending pleasure ride, pushing for more and more and more.

"I'm close," I say urgently, and he backs off. I grip his hair, desperate, canting my hips up.

He lifts his head. "I want to play with you more."

I whimper as he laps gently. Oh God, I'm so achy and needy. I need him to fill me. I need release. I lift my head, propping up on my elbows. "Cal, please."

He smiles, pushes me flat on my back, and continues the sweet torture. I collapse, throwing my arms wide in complete surrender. He immediately ratchets up the pace, the pressure. My surrender unleashes the beast.

My head thrashes on the pillow as the room fades from view, my senses dimming except for the white-hot pleasure at my center as Cal owns my body. He crooks his finger, pressing up at the same time as he takes and takes and takes. The release slams into me, and I cry out, bucking against his hold. He keeps me close, guiding me through wave after wave of pleasure until I'm spent.

He shifts away. I hear the rustle of the condom wrapper from my nightstand, and then he's back, sliding deep into me. He groans into my neck. I wrap my arms and legs around him. Finally, the empty ache is filled.

He lifts his head and kisses me. "So good. It's so good with you."

"It's us."

He starts to move, keeping a slow and steady rhythm, pushing as deep as he can go. He slides a hand under my hip and angles me up to take more of him. Something about the angle hits just right. I grab his ass and pull him closer, needing more. He gives me exactly what I need, pumping hard and fast, both of us racing to release. My climax hits in a rush, my insides clasping him rhythmically.

He lets go of his tight control, pounding into me until his own release hits. He throws his head back with a groan. A few moments later, he shifts to collapse next to me on the bed.

I turn off the bedside lamp and flop back on the mattress, too spent to do anything but float in the aftermath of pleasure. Long moments pass in mutual blissed-out exhaustion.

Eventually, he pulls me into his side, and I rest my head on his chest with a satisfied smile.

He kisses my hair. "How long do you think it'll take to get each other out of our systems?"

Out of our systems?

The words are like a splash of cold water. This is just sex for him. I'm the best person *for sex*. I'm such an idiot, reading into something that wasn't there.

I turn the bedside lamp back on and stare down at him. "What do you mean get each other out of our systems?"

"All this crazy sex. Eventually, we'll get it all out of our systems."

I clench my jaw.

"Probably take a long time," he adds.

I speak through my teeth. "I'm thinking now. Now is when we get it out of our systems."

He props up on his elbows. "Now?"

"You should go. This was a mistake."

He looks at me for a long moment. "Okay."

I watch as he dresses, and then I watch him walk out the door, anger and tears battling it out inside me.

Tears win.

13

———

I drag myself to our weekly meeting on Monday. Saturday night with Cal was a huge mistake. I should've listened to my instincts. I set a clear boundary for the whole fake-dating thing—no sex. And then I totally initiated just because he said I was the best person he ever met. I exhale sharply, more mad at myself than him. I knew better. I knew I was playing with fire, and this is what happens, I got burned.

I need time away from him, and then he'll be out of *my* system. Hmph. I still can't believe he said that. There I was feeling so close to him when he was thinking of the end. It's fine. He works on a street that I can easily avoid, and there's absolutely no reason for me to make the three-block walk to his apartment. I'll stick to my usual places, and eventually this will all get easier.

I open the back door that leads to our office. At least at work, I've got Nathan and Owen to keep me on my toes.

Climbing the stairs to our rented space above Something's Brewing Café, I mentally review today's agenda. I breeze through the kitchen into the main room we use as a meeting space and come to a screeching halt. *No!*

Cal's here in all his tall, broad-shouldered athlete physique glory. Those big competent hands. The sexy memories are too fresh. What is he doing here? I need time and lots of space away from him.

I look away, willing myself to stop flushing hot. He's talking to Nathan like they're best pals. When did that happen?

I set my satchel on the table, ignoring the pounding of my heart. "Morning. Where's Owen?"

Nathan scratches his dark stubbled jaw. "Doctor appointment. He'll be back soon. You remember Cal the lawyer?"

Cal inclines his head, looking more handsome than any man has a right to be in a crisp white dress shirt. *Dammit! He's not supposed to be here!*

Cal turns to Nathan. "Usually people say Cal the baseball player, so lawyer's nice to hear."

Nathan says, "Ball player usually has better status, except with the odd ones like Mackenzie here. Not a fan of America's pastime. Unless you buy her a hot dog and a beer."

"Only in it for the snacks," Cal says, which he already knows from our movie marathon. "Fair enough. I'm the same way with romantic comedies. Need a popcorn and Milk Duds to sit through one of those."

I take a seat and boot up my laptop. I work to keep a neutral professional voice. "Why do we need a lawyer?"

"Don't knock those movies," Nathan says to Cal. "Best way to a woman's heart. Besides chocolate, that is."

They share a chuckle, and now I want to punch someone. We're not here to talk about women or hearts. This is so stupid.

I try another tactic. "We don't need a lawyer."

Nathan pulls out a seat and gestures for Cal to do the same. "I'd like some legal advice for that conflict of interest."

I thought our meeting today was to decide which client was more important to keep. We couldn't find a workaround. I guess that's where Cal comes in. I have to rise above the personal and consider what's best for our business. Even when every cell in my body is telling me to run.

Or shove Cal out the door. I'm surprisingly strong for my size.

Nathan studies me. "You're okay with Cal, right? There's no kind of conflict of interest between you two."

"Of course not!" I say hotly and immediately want to sink into the floor and keep going into the magma of the Earth's core.

"I used to do corporate work, so I've seen this situation before," Cal says.

Oh, okay, so we're going to pretend it's completely normal that we're now working together after I kicked him out of bed? For good reason! Cool, cool. No problem here.

"Mackenzie?" Nathan gives me a searching look. "Did you hear me?"

I stare at him blankly. "Say again."

"The contracts for our clients."

I pull them up on my laptop and address Cal's eyebrow, unable to meet his eyes without imploding. "What's your email? I'll send you the contracts we have with them both."

"Already got them from Nathan," Cal says, giving me a strange look.

"Can you go over it with him?" Nathan asks patiently. "I have to go visit another potential client in the financial district."

A zip of pure panic races up my spine. Alone with Cal? No, no, no. "We'll reschedule for a better time. What potential client?"

Nathan stands and grabs his jacket, putting it on. "Someone I found on my own this weekend during basketball. I've been working all the angles."

I stare at him imploringly. "Nathan, wait."

He slaps Cal on the shoulder. "You're in good hands here with Mackenzie. She basically runs the place."

"So she told me," Cal says with a grin.

Nathan barks out a laugh and strides to the door. I nearly topple over my chair in my hurry to catch up to him. I grab him by the sleeve before he gets to the door.

He turns. "What's wrong? You look like somebody ran over your cat."

"Never say that! Felix is the best cat ever." I lower my voice. "Listen, you can't leave me here with him. I'm unprepared. You should've run this by me first."

"It's no big deal. You know the clients inside out. Just answer his questions. We're lucky he's not charging us by the hour. I worked out a project fee that's very reasonable. He's trying to build goodwill here in town."

He reaches for the door, and I plaster myself against it. "Reschedule your other meeting."

"What is wrong…oh." He gives me a knowing look. "You slept with him."

"Shh!"

He pats my shoulder. "Good for you."

"I ended it," I whisper fiercely. "Now it's awkward as hell. I can't work like this. You need to take this on at another time."

He looks perplexed, his brows crinkling together. "Ended what? Was it, like, a relationship? Don't you usually have a *carefully outlined with all the rules* fling?"

I bristle at his teasing. It's my organized, rule-following nature that keeps this place running. "It's none of your business. I just want to reschedule for a better time when you and Owen can be here."

He gives me a look bordering on pity. "Mackenzie, from a guy's perspective, he's over it. Did you see how relaxed he was in there? He's fine. So you'll be fine too."

I grit my teeth. "I am fine."

He smiles, showing both dimples. "Good. Then you can manage to work on one small project together. He'll probably bore you to tears with all the legalese, and all that pent-up lust you're holding onto will vanish."

I purse my lips. "I don't have pent-up lust." *I'm way too satisfied for that, which is not the point. Focus!*

He lifts his palms. "No judgment. Now if you'll excuse me, I really do need to get to this meeting."

I reluctantly move away from the door. He makes a quick exit.

I turn back and stride into the room. Cal's looking out the window at Main Street. The view across the way is Happy Endings bar, the site of our first kiss. My mind flashes to strong arms lifting me, the all-consuming kiss as he pressed me against the door, all of the hard planes of his body deliciously meeting my soft aching places.

My shoulders sag. I'm doomed. Every time I see him, I'm going to have a highlight reel of our sexy times running through my brain. That's why I had no plans to see him.

He turns. "Everything okay?"

"You know what? Let's get Sutton in on this by video chat. That way I don't have to bring her up to speed later."

"Sure."

Cal closes the distance, facing me across the meeting room table. My gaze roams from his serious expression to the column of his neck to his wide shoulders, that chest. My mouth is dry.

I take a seat. "I'll get Sutton on chat." He doesn't seem upset in the aftermath of Saturday night. It just proves it meant nothing to him beyond the physical. I'm so mad at myself. I fell for him. I did, even when every instinct told me to keep my guard up. My eyes get hot. Do *not* cry.

"You want me to call her?" Cal asks, taking the seat adjacent to me.

I shake my head and connect with Sutton a few moments later. As soon as she answers, I turn the screen so we can both see her. "Hi, Sutton, I've got Cal here with me today. We're going to be working on that conflict of interest I mentioned. I thought you should be in the loop."

Sutton, a pretty brunette with a bright smile, waves at us. "Hi! What a surprise. I didn't know Cal would be working with us. Didn't I tell you Mackenzie was beautiful and smart too?"

"You did," Cal says warmly.

Now I'm warm. I'm not used to compliments like that.

Well, Cal didn't give me a compliment. His sister did. "Let's get down to business."

"You two have so much in common," Sutton says.

"We do?" Cal asks.

I rub my temple. Sutton is starting to remind me of my matchmaking mom. The last thing I need when I'm trying to protect my heart.

Sutton starts ticking off our compatibility with her fingers. "Both from small towns, both veered from your first careers, and you're both Hufflepuffs."

My cheeks flush. Cal sends me an amused look.

I clear my throat. "I'm not sure what you mean by that but okay. I've got the—"

"Hufflepuffs are kind, loyal, and hardworking," Sutton says. "You do so know. You've read the Harry Potter series more than I have."

I rub the side of my neck. "When I was a kid. I feel like we're getting off topic."

"And Cal's read them too."

"I said the movies are cool," Cal says. "I'm not actively participating in hufflepuffing."

I smile despite my sour mood.

"What about your—" Sutton starts.

Cal cuts her off. "Okay, back to business."

"He has a wand," Sutton whispers.

I'd laugh, but I have one too. He sends me an embarrassed look.

"We don't need to talk about this ever again," I say. "Sutton, please take notes. Cal, let's start with the nondisclosure section of the agreement."

We get to work. Cal puts on reading glasses, and I pretend not to notice how sexy he looks with them as he displays all his legal competence. He's all business, which is exactly what I'll be for the rest of this work arrangement.

I'm going to kill Nathan and Owen for springing this on me.

When we wrap up, I stand, ready to make my escape, but

no-o-o. Cal appears by my side. "Mackenzie, wait. I don't think the other night was a mistake."

I press my lips in a flat line, steeling myself against any treacherous sweetness. I won't be fooled again.

"We have good chemistry," he says.

I grab my satchel. "Ah, yes. Chemistry. And don't forget friendship."

He snags my wrist, his thumb stroking the soft underside. I yank my wrist out of reach.

"It's a start," he says. "Maybe—"

I meet his eyes, keeping my voice neutral. "Are you saying you want a relationship?"

He hesitates. And there's my answer.

"I'm not sure what I'm saying," he says. "The fake dating doesn't feel fake anymore."

"Why?"

He opens his mouth and closes it again.

"You told me you're not good at relationships," I say in a matter-of-fact tone like it doesn't bother me in the least.

He clears his throat. "I'm not."

"And you just got out of a serious relationship that ended badly. I'm not saying that was your fault, but it seems too soon for you to jump into something new. If that is what you're hinting at. I can't tell, and I don't want to guess anymore."

His brows draw together, but he says nothing.

I force a smile. "It's fine. Really. A little space between us would be good before we can try being friends again, okay?"

"You're the one who came on to me," he says.

I suck in air. "Bye, Cal."

I drag myself through the week. Thankfully, the rest of the work project with *what's-his-name*, whom I am not thinking about, is through email. Nathan said he'll take the final meeting with *what's-his-name* to review the papers that need signing since I handled the first meeting. Now it's Thursday night, and I've hit an all-time low, finishing off a pint of Ben & Jerry's chocolate chip cookie dough ice cream for dinner.

Harper's not home, and she didn't respond to my text. One of the nice things about growing up with Harper was finally having a sister to commiserate with. We were outnumbered at home with two brothers each. I count on her for this kind of misery.

I'm sick of wallowing. I grab my coat and head for Happy Endings. I'll get a bite to eat of real food at the bar and be around people.

When I get there, my brother Cooper is bartending. He resembles Dad, tall with brown hair and brown eyes. He's mischievous like Dad, but also empathetic like Mom. That's probably why distressed women drinking at the bar always used to share their problems with him. He became known as the rescuer of women. Rowan put her foot down, and now he's friendly with distressed women, but no longer on rescue duty.

"Hey, big sis," he says. "Is this a white wine or mojito night?"

"Wine, thanks."

He grabs my favorite wine from the refrigerator and pours me a glass. "Everything okay? You don't seem like your usual cheerful self."

"I'm cheerful."

He gives me a look as he hands over the glass. "Try again."

I take a long swallow of wine. "Why do men suck?"

"Uh-oh."

"Yeah."

He leans across the bar. "You should tell it to the crowd across the street."

"What crowd?"

"The Happy Endings Book Club. They meet tonight. I'm surprised you're not over there now. Rowan and Harper are there."

A stab of betrayal hits my already bruised heart. And, okay, a little bit of FOMO. This is why Harper couldn't be there for me in my misery. She fell in with the romance crowd behind my back. Meanwhile, I share every little thing in my life with her. She used to say she didn't believe in all that love fantasy stuff after her live-in boyfriend of two years cheated on her *in their bed*. What about that, huh? We were a united anti-love front.

And another thing she never shared—she never told me why she's always pissy with Nathan all these years. I tell her *everything*.

Does this mean Harper's going to start looking for a happy-ever-after fantasy man and leave me behind? We were supposed to be roomies for at least our fun twenties. That was the plan.

And since when does Rowan read romance? When I first met Rowan, she had a decidedly anti-romance stance. How my brother Cooper managed to turn that around is a mystery to me. I guess being the new partner in Mom's wedding planning business finally got to her.

That book club is filled with Mom and her friends, all my favorite aunties, and now my friends are there without me. This is so wrong.

I toss back the rest of my wine. "Put it on my tab." I hop off the bar stool and march toward the door.

"Dude, it's free for family," Cooper calls after me.

"I know!"

I shove the door open and jog across the street to Something's Brewing Café.

~

Cal

I thought I would feel out of place, but this romance book club has been very welcoming. When Mad invited me last week, I looked up the book on the store's event calendar. At the time I thought it could be one of those fake-date things for me and Mackenzie. Then, of course, I had to actually read the book so I wasn't lost during the discussion.

Fiery Embrace was an eye-opener. First, I had no idea there were sex scenes in these books. My little sister reads them voraciously. Explains more than I want to know. Second, I finally understand a woman's thoughts and feelings. It was all spelled out right there. I can't believe more guys haven't caught on to this.

The women's animated talk at the café fades into the background as I review what happened with Mackenzie again to figure out where it went wrong. We had a great night. I said the wrong thing, as I often do, but what was wrong with what I said? It would take a long time to get each other out of our systems is a good thing. And good chemistry means I like being with her.

She took everything the wrong way. Then she put me in the *maybe sometime in the future* friend zone. Friends! After all we shared.

For the first time in my life, I don't know the next strategic move. All these confusing feelings cloud my thinking. I want to stuff them down into the box that holds all my unwanted feelings, but they're too strong for that.

And then suddenly she's here. The blood rushes through my veins. Our eyes meet across the room, her lips forming a perfect O of surprise.

Shit. She's going to think I'm not giving her space like she asked. Should I bail? I'm sitting in a circle of women. It would draw a lot of attention if I suddenly stood and left.

Her gaze shifts, riveted on Harper. Mackenzie does not look happy with her. A temporary reprieve for me. I need to come up with a good explanation for being here that doesn't let on how clueless I am about the emotional lives of women. *Think!*

14

Mackenzie

I'm trying really hard to keep my shit together, but not only are Harper and Rowan here behind my back, but Cal's here too. And why else would he be here? Mom must've invited him after I told her not to do any more matchmaking with him! Or anyone!

Oh, wait, she didn't know I'd be here. What the hell is Cal doing here?

I stand there, waiting for a break in the conversation. The women and Cal sit in a circle in the center of the room, the tables pushed against the walls. I glance around at the lively group, Mom and some of my favorite aunties, Mad, Lauren, Charlotte, and Carrie. Aunt Ally isn't here, still on her cruise around the world. She'd be the one to make me feel better about not believing in romance. She's the one who discovered sologamy and married herself as part of her single-me, happy-me plan. She always said romance was a fantasy. Of course, that was before she fell madly in love and married Uncle Ethan.

I blink back tears. I don't know why I'm so upset. It's just a book. Why do I care if everyone is into romance except me?

Aunt Mad is fervently defending the heroine for hooking

up with the hero again after their breakup. I don't dare look at Cal. Don't draw any comparisons, nothing like us.

"Obviously the breakup was temporary," Harper says. "They're locked in, so hooking up was fine by me. Also, hello? Steamy as hell."

"Harper, what are you doing here?" I burst out.

All eyes turn to me. Cal brings a chair over for me next to Harper, and the women make room.

"Thank you." I take a seat and turn to Harper. "You like this happy-ever-after stuff?" My voice drops to a whisper, my eyes stinging. "Why didn't you tell me?"

She rolls her eyes. "It's no big deal. It's fun like those black-and-white movies your mom turned me onto."

Mom smiles. "They are fun. So nice to see you, sweetie, and your boyfriend too."

Obviously she believes the fake-dating thing and thinks nothing of it. I spent all that time with Cal to prove a point, and then I was the one to fall in love. Me, Miss Practical. I try to smile but can't manage it.

Mom continues, smiling at Cal, "We always find the male perspective on romance enlightening."

The women snicker, giving each other significant looks. I wonder if they make their husbands read romance.

"It held my interest," Cal says. "There was a lot of unexpected stuff in there. All good, though."

My eyes widen. *Seriously? Is he talking about sex with my female family and friends?*

He continues in an amiable tone, "I already started book two in the series."

The women applaud. I shrink into my seat, feeling like an outsider.

"The steam level was on point," Aunt Mad says.

"Oh my God, the elevator scene," Harper says.

"What did you think about the bathroom scene?" Mom asks the group.

"See, I don't find that sexy anymore," Aunt Charlotte says. "Germs."

"Can we assume the fictional bathroom has been properly sanitized?" Aunt Carrie asks.

Everyone laughs. Cal launches into a serious discussion of the romance genre and what it means to women and how that reflects on men and our culture as a whole. Next thing you know, my cat is going to start walking on his hind legs and telling me he wants a forever love.

Seeing Cal take seriously what these women love gets to me. My anger fades, and warmth takes its place. Maybe one day we can be friends again. He's a good person, just not good for me.

I zone out until people start gathering their coats and purses. Cal stands and holds out my coat to help me into it. It's more trouble than it's worth to avoid him, so I slide my arms into the sleeves, feeling Mom's eyes on me.

A few moments later, we walk out the door, heading to Happy Endings across the street for drinks. Aunt Mad joins Cal, telling him he should meet her sons, who are big baseball fans. They start talking baseball.

I get a step behind, and Mom joins me. "I was surprised to see you and Cal here."

I can't take my eyes off Cal in profile as he speaks to Aunt Mad. He's so handsome and well spoken. I wish I didn't notice everything about him. "Yeah, uh…" Then I remember Aunt Mad invited us both last week. Cal must've taken Aunt Mad's invitation seriously, and how sweet is it that he wants to be part of things? "Aunt Mad invited us."

Cal smiles at something Aunt Mad says, and my pulse skitters.

"So things are going well between you two?" Mom asks gently.

Is this the point where I confess we were fake dating, or do I say we broke up? Did we break up?

"Mmm. He's good. So how's work?"

"We've got our spring and summer fully booked."

"That's great."

"Yeah. Oh! We're planning a girls' trip to New Orleans

after the busy season," Mom says. "Harper's going. You're welcome to join us."

Yet another thing Harper never shared. She's got new hobbies, a new outlook on love, and a girls' trip in the works. What kind of best friend/sister/cousin leaves you out of so much of their life?

"Mackenzie, are you okay?" Mom asks.

"I'm fine. Sounds fun. Text me the dates, and I'll see if I can make it work."

Cal opens the door to Happy Endings for all of us, earning him many smiles and thank yous from the other women. I sigh. It's maddening how he can be both sweet and distressing at the same time.

A few guys at the dark cherrywood bar watch basketball on the big-screen TV. They glance back at the din of women talking and laughing as they filter in and shift to the end of the bar. I hang back with Cal.

"Are you into romance novels now?" I ask.

He shrugs. "I was curious. I didn't come to stalk you or anything. Do you want me to leave?"

"No, you don't have to leave."

"I was invited to your parents' vow-renewal ceremony. Is that going to be a problem?"

I bite my lower lip. It's not going to be easy to avoid Cal, though I'm starting to wonder why I want to. "No problem here."

He leans close to whisper, "Your mom and friends think we're still together from our fake dating. How do you want to play this?"

I look to the ceiling, considering. I've been miserable all week.

On the other hand, how am I ever going to move on if I keep pretending we're a couple? I turn to him, my shoe somehow scuffing on the floor, sending me off balance. He reaches out to steady me. We're close, the heat spiking between us.

I swallow hard. "You don't have to play my boyfriend

anymore."

He brushes a lock of hair behind my ear, his dark eyes warm on mine. My heart thumps harder. "What if I like it?" He tips my chin up and kisses me. A tender kiss that's over before I can blink. It shakes the foundation of all my firm principles meant to protect my heart.

I'm in trouble.

"I love when you look at me like that," he says, his lips curving up in a smile that can only be described as sexy beyond belief, tender, and affectionate all rolled into one.

I look away, taking a breath. Sex is what got me into this mess. I need to slow it down.

The women get louder. I turn to find Aunt Mad high-fiving her friends. Harper's in the middle of it all. She waves me over. I walk over with Cal just as Rowan comes up behind me. Was Harper calling Rowan over and not me? Why do I feel left behind again?

"Hey, ladies!" Rowan says, giving Harper and then me a hug. "Are we all joining the Happy Endings Book Club? Mackenzie, you in?"

"You read romance now?" I ask.

"Not yet, but I do read historical fiction, and Harper told me the next book is historical."

"Scottish Highlander romance," Harper says. "You should see the cover. The kilt on this guy."

Rowan laughs. I glance sideways at Cal to see how he's taking all this talk about guys. He kisses my temple. It's so easy to fall for him.

"Want anything to drink?" he asks.

"I'll take a mojito," I say. He looks to my friends.

"Sparkling water, please," Rowan says.

"Merlot for me, thanks," Harper says.

Cal makes his way to bartender Cooper while Harper, Rowan, and I shift over to a high-top table. "So…" I say, unsure how to proceed. *Is everyone having romance fun without me?*

"Are you pregnant?" Harper asks Rowan at the same time

as Rowan asks me, "Are you and Cal a couple?"

"What?" Rowan and I say at the same time.

"Wait," Harper says. "Rowan, what's up with the sparkling water?"

She lifts one shoulder. "Cooper and I are doing this seventy-day challenge for clean eating, exercise, and meditation. If I don't make it the seventy days, I have to do laundry duty for the next seventy days, and if he doesn't make it the seventy days, he has to meal plan, grocery shop, cook, and clean up the dishes for the next seventy days."

My jaw drops. "Whoa, you guys are hard-core."

"His loss sounds much harder than yours," Harper says.

Rowan shrugs. "That's how much he wants me to do this with him. He gave me incredible motivation."

"And if you both make it the seventy days, what do you win?" I ask.

"We win at life," she says with a straight face.

Harper and I laugh. "No, really," Harper says.

Rowan smiles. "Really. Okay, Cooper came up with that, but I'm on board. Plus we'll be looking good for our honeymoon in St. Bart's." She turns to me. "So you and Cal, huh?"

"I knew you weren't just friends," Harper says. "Movies and cuddling is relationship territory."

"Aww," Rowan says. "That's so sweet. What movie?"

"Back up. Why are you two suddenly into romance?" I ask.

"Cooper made me believe," Rowan says with a dreamy smile.

Harper shrugs. "It's fun. And I didn't tell you because I knew you'd be all judgy."

I huff. "Because we made fun of this club. We agreed it was all fake and gave women high expectations that could never be met."

"Maybe my expectations were too low," Harper says. "You have high expectations even without those books, but I never did."

"You did all this behind my back," I say, unable to keep

the hurt from my voice.

"You did all this Cal stuff behind my back," she says.

"I told you what was up," I say between my teeth.

"Right. You left out some important stuff."

"Like what?"

Rowan wrinkles her nose. "Didn't your mom warn you away from him since he's a player?"

"What does that even mean?" Harper asks. "The man had a live-in relationship."

"What's the deal with him?" Rowan asks.

A rush of emotions bombards me at once—his soulful eyes, the way he talks to me and really listens, the fun we have together. How I'm falling for him, and he's still just having fun. Casual.

What the hell am I doing kissing him and letting him do all his gallant stuff like we're right back where we were? We can never be there again because I have *feelings* and he doesn't. He made that clear when I asked him if he wanted a relationship. His silence was damning. And then he accused me of being the one to initiate, which, let's face it, I did. I have to stop. Why can't I stop?

I speak in a rush, trying to outrun the panic. "He's fun, but I'd never want to be in a relationship with someone like him."

Harper and Rowan stare over my shoulder with twin looks of horror. The hair on the back of my neck rises. I wince. He's behind me, isn't he?

I turn. Cal avoids eye contact, setting our drinks down on the table without a word. He definitely heard that.

I swallow hard. "Cal, I—"

"I'm going to get a beer." His voice is flat, devoid of all emotion.

He leaves. My stomach drops. What do I say? He told me he wasn't good at relationships, so it's true I wouldn't want to push for that.

Harper gives me a look filled with pity. "You know, I think you could learn a lot from reading romance."

I drop my head in my hands and groan. "Not helpful."

15

I'm fine. I'm really, really fine. Ugh, I'm so not fine. It's been a week, and I can't stop replaying what happened with Cal at Happy Endings. He stayed away for the rest of the night, drinking his beer at the bar, talking to Aunt Charlotte and Aunt Lauren. And now he's ghosted me. Won't return my calls or texts. I'm not going to beg.

What does he expect me to say? *I'm sorry, I actually would like to be in a relationship with you.* Is that what he wants? He sure has a funny way of showing it.

How can I make this better? Then I remember we made a deal. He said he'd do the fake-dating thing, and in return, I'd get his sister, Sutton, to move here for a job. That has to get him to talk to me again. Besides, I've been wanting Sutton in a larger role.

"Mackenzie, thoughts?" Nathan asks.

We're having an in-office meeting, and I'm spacing out, convincing myself I'm fine. "New client wants more hands-on from you. Let's work up the scope and billable hours."

Nathan and Owen exchange a look. "Yes, but," Nathan says slowly, "I'm asking what you think about me moving to an apartment in the city to build my network with the financial sector. Now that we've snagged one client, it could help.

A lot goes on after hours in the city. It would mean I'd be less available for these in-person meetings."

"And so he can meet women," Owen adds helpfully.

"Would you shut up about that?" Nathan says with no real heat. "Meeting women has never been a problem for me."

"Ah, but the *right* woman could require a larger pool to choose from," Owen says. He's one of those happily married people who thinks everyone should get married. I'd find it irritating if I weren't so happy for him and Shayla.

"I thought you loved your house in Eastman," I say.

"I do," Nathan says. "I decided to keep it as a place to take a break from the city."

"Sure." Sometimes I forget he comes from money. He's an only child with a trust fund. His family founded a major financial services company generations ago. That company isn't our client because Nathan's dad, while tolerant of his son's entrepreneurism, ultimately expects him to join the family company. In other words, he's not making it easy on Nathan. All the connections Nathan has with the financial sector have been with the sons and daughters of his dad's friends. That younger generation is more open to tech security as a priority.

I nod. "We'll make do with you on video calls, emails, texts."

"Great."

"I'd like to bring Sutton on in a larger role," I say. "If she accepts my offer, we'd have her here in person a couple of days a week as an office manager with the potential to grow into a client manager for new-client setup and outreach to existing clients. She's fast and accurate researching new clients and industries. A real asset to the team."

"You want her to move here?" Owen asks. "Can we afford that? Cost-of-living raise plus a greater role means more money."

"And benefits," Nathan says. "She wouldn't be a contractor anymore."

"Since we didn't lose that client to a conflict of interest, and with Nathan's new client and a few cost-saving measures, I think she'll pay for herself in six months."

"What cost-saving measures?" Nathan asks.

"I'm working on locking in the rent here in exchange for a longer lease, and bumping our rates for new clients."

"Finance clients can afford it," Nathan says. "But it's no guarantee I can bring them in."

"Half those guys are friends of your dad's," Owen says. "They're an easy reach, and I don't know why you were so against approaching them in the first place."

"Because I wanted to stand on my own two feet like you," Nathan says. "Now that we're more established, it makes sense to branch out."

"If it doesn't work out with Sutton's additional cost, I'll take a pay cut," I say.

Owen and Nathan stare at me like I'm crazy.

"Why would you do that?" Nathan asks.

"That's how much I believe in Sutton's value to the company." And I promised Cal I'd do my best to bring her here with a job offer. That was our deal. Cal didn't renege on his part of the deal, and I won't either. Even if things are weird between us right now. Or more like nonexistent.

Owen slaps the table. "Why not? Let's take a risk. It's only money. We'll make more."

"That's the spirit," I say.

Nathan lifts his to-go coffee cup. "What's the point of owning your own business if you're not willing to take risks? Bring Sutton on."

Cal

I wrap up with my client, feeling good about bringing in someone new. Perry wants to set up a corporation for a dog-grooming business. Corporate setup is in my wheelhouse, unlike my other cases so far—a property dispute over garbage-can placement, a landlord-tenant situation gone bad, and a ferret owner accused of not abiding by the local leash law. I'm liking the variety in my new job.

I shake Perry's hand. "Best of luck. I'll be in touch for next steps."

She smiles, her brightly colored orange hair making her look like the sun. "Great! Bye, Cal. Thanks for helping me through the legalese."

"That's what I'm here for."

She lets herself out the door. My phone rings, and I check the screen. Sutton. Adrenaline races through me. Something must be wrong. We text a lot more than we talk on the phone. Is Dad having one of his depressive episodes? Sometimes he can't get out of bed and misses work.

I answer. "Everything okay?"

"Yes, everything's fine," she says. "I'm fine. Dad's fine."

I let out a breath. "Okay, what's up?"

"I don't know what to do."

I sit on the end of my desk. "Okay," I say slowly, giving her time to share. I swear if her crap boyfriend did something, I'll be on the next flight out to kick his ass.

"Mackenzie made me a great job offer to go from assistant to office manager with the potential to grow into a client-facing role. And I'd get stock!"

My jaw drops. I didn't think Mackenzie would follow through with the job offer since I didn't see the whole fake-dating thing through. How could I when she can't stand the idea of being with someone like me? Those were her exact words. *Someone like him.* Obviously she thinks I'm not good enough for her, exactly like her mom said from the start.

But then that same night she looked at me with so much warmth I thought she wanted to be with me. I never would've kissed her again if I thought she was done with me. This is so confusing. I wish I could stop thinking about her.

"Cal?"

"Yeah, uh, congratulations on your job. That's great."

"Thanks. It's a nice bump in pay, and I love working with

her and Nathan and Owen. Your boss and coworkers can make all the difference in a work environment. I'm not sure I'd ever find a better work situation."

"Uh-huh." I wait patiently for her to spit out the problem, though I already know. She'd have to leave her loser boyfriend behind.

She goes on detailing the responsibilities as per the offer Mackenzie sent her.

"The problem is, she says it's a hybrid position. I'd need to be in-office twice a week and can be remote the rest of the week."

"That's pretty common nowadays. Clover Park is a nice town. I'm here, and you already know Mackenzie, Nathan, and Owen. Ask Mackenzie to introduce you to her mom, Hailey. She's a master networker in town. She'll introduce you to so many people it'll make your head spin. In a good way. You'll feel comfortable in no time."

There's a pause. I tell myself to be cool about what I know is coming next.

She lowers her voice. "I've been waiting for John to propose. If I move away, he definitely won't."

I pinch the bridge of my nose. "You could stay there for years and he might never propose. Are you going to put your life on hold for a hypothetical proposal?"

"I don't have to take the job. I'm perfectly fine being a virtual assistant. And Dad—"

"You said Dad's fine."

"He is, but you know how he gets."

It strikes me how unfair it's been for Sutton living at home. After Mom died, Sutton dedicated herself to taking care of Dad in his grief, but she was grieving too. She and Mom were close. I was in college at the time so wasn't there to help day to day; then I played ball, followed by law school. I had my own life while Sutton's life stayed on hold.

"Dad's a grown man," I say.

"But he'll be all alone."

"He can join a club or something, or finally seek help.

Maybe having you there makes it too easy for him to do nothing. Maybe it's best for him if you move on with your life."

Dad refuses to try antidepressants. Mom's death was basically the end of his life. I've lost a lot too, but I'm not depressed. I built a life for myself.

Sutton speaks softly. "I don't know, Cal. I think he needs me."

I take a deep breath. "Sure, status quo is always an option. Or you could get in on the ground floor of a company with the potential to grow. Maybe take a few community college classes."

"College is expensive," she says as she always does. It's been fifteen years since Mom died, and I don't want Sutton to permanently put her life on hold taking care of Dad and hoping her boyfriend proposes one day. I want her to have options. She's brilliant. She could do so much more with her life.

"That's what scholarships and financial aid are for."

"I don't know. This move seems too risky."

"If it's a mistake, you can always go home again. Right?"

"John and I have been together for eight years now. That's a long time. We were high school sweethearts like Mom and Dad."

But you're not like Mom and Dad because John cheats on you.

I take a slow breath. It takes a huge effort to stay calm and reasonable when I just want her to see what a scum he is. "Why don't you have a talk with him? See if he's on the same page about your future together. Better to know now if he's not thinking about marriage after eight years."

"Right. Like every guy wants to be pressured into marriage."

"Look, you called me so you must want my advice. Do what's best for you and your career. Opportunities like this don't come up that often. Accept the job, try it out. If you find after six months to a year that it's not a good fit, then you can always go home again."

"I guess."

Inspiration strikes. "There's a romance book club and a bookstore." I don't mention that I joined them. That would invite too many questions, and I'm not about to explain my new interest in understanding women's emotions, courtesy of Mackenzie and our complicated relationship.

I still. A relationship. Did this casual-turned-fake-dating thing turn into something real? It snuck up on me. And that's why everything got messed up. Because I suck at the feelings part.

"A bookstore and a romance book club! Wow. I've always wanted to be in a romance book club. Every book club I found out here reads depressing books. I can't believe Mackenzie never mentioned it."

"I don't think she reads romance, but her mom is the leader of it."

"That must've been so nice growing up with a romance-loving mom."

"She's a great lady. You'll like her."

"I'm sure I will. Ack! Am I really doing this? Moving halfway across the country for a new job?"

"It's a great opportunity, and you earned it."

"I'll see if John's willing to do long distance for a while. This doesn't have to be forever."

"Exactly."

"Okay, thanks, Cal! Love you!"

"Love you too."

She hangs up.

I smile at her cheery bye. I'm glad she's excited about the job because her relationship is a dead end. Big picture, she'll be much happier moving on with her life.

Mackenzie

I walk idly down Main Street for the big Clover Park side-walk sale, hoping a little shopping will lift my spirits. It's the end of March, and the sidewalk sale is one of the ways the local businesses try to get more foot traffic. People shop while enjoying the music of the local band, Reverb, made up of the high school music teacher, his friends, and some students doing covers of music from the eighties.

I check out a cute boutique's selection of spring dresses and sense someone staring. Cal just came out of Happy Endings. He waves. At least I get a wave after more than a week of ghosting. I give him a quick wave, feeling awkward and overheated, and go back to shopping. I didn't expect him to come out for the Saturday sidewalk sale.

I glance across the street again but don't see him. Guess I don't have to worry about awkward conversation, though I would like to apologize for what he overheard before. I was in super-defensive mode with Harper and Rowan peppering me with Cal questions. I turn to go and walk right into a solid chest.

I jump back. "Cal!"

"You made Sutton an offer even though I didn't fulfill my end of the bargain."

I stuff my hands in my pockets. "It had nothing to do with our bargain. Sutton's a valuable employee."

"It's a big step forward for her life. Just don't tell her it was part of our deal. Can I buy you ice cream as a thank you? Heard it's the best in the state."

He ghosts me, and now he acts like nothing ever happened. I can't let this one go.

"Listen, Cal, I'm sorry about what I said before. I didn't mean it the way it sounded about being in a relationship with someone like you. You're great, just not...well, you said you're not good at relationships, and you just got out of one, so—"

"Don't worry about it."

"You seemed upset. You didn't text me back."

"I needed some space to get things straight in my head. So ice cream with a friend?"

I tilt my head. "Are we friends?"

"Why not?"

Oh, so many reasons. Let's see—hookups one through ten; I find you irresistibly sexy and charming and smart.

And I'm stupid in love with you.

He smiles. "Come on, one scoop. On me."

"Sure."

We walk towards Shane's Scoops, passing more sidewalk-sales racks and tables. The sidewalks are decorated with colorful chalk drawings. Kids always help decorate for local events.

"How've you been?" he asks.

"Fine. Sutton's excited about coming out here and joining the Happy Endings Book Club. If I'd known that was a selling point, I would've mentioned it early on. I'm so glad she took our offer."

"Her boyfriend is giving her a hard time about leaving. He said if she leaves, it's goodbye forever."

"So how did she decide to let him go? They've been together for a long time, right?"

"He didn't want to get married. That's all the answer she needed. She's upset but also eager to move on and get a change of scenery."

"Then it all worked out."

He opens the door to Shane's Scoops, and we join the line. The handwritten chalk menu declares the specials—chocolate brownie, peanut butter swirl, and mocha—and then there's the usual lineup of awesome flavors.

"Let me guess, you like chocolate," he says.

"Chocolate brownie. Double the chocolate. Let me guess yours—strawberry."

"Nope."

"Mint?"

He grins. "Nope."

"Here I thought I knew you so well after fake dating."

He shifts closer. "Don't forget the week when—"

"We were getting to know each other."

He searches my expression. I face front. Not going there.

Cal peers at the label in the case. "Oh good, they have it."

"Butter pecan?"

"Vanilla."

I stare at him. "You were worried they wouldn't have the most basic of flavors?"

"Basic? Vanilla is the best. Subtle but flavorful. It doesn't hit you over the head to have a good time. Sort of sneaks up on you and lingers."

He gives me a lopsided smile. My knees weaken. Does he want to linger?

A boy around four years old turns from the counter with his cookies-and-cream cone, takes a giant lick, and the scoop promptly rolls off the cone and splats on the floor. "No-o-o-o!" he cries.

His dad is wrestling a baby into a stroller. "Just pick it up and put it back," his dad says.

"It's dirty!"

"We don't have time. We have to get to your sister's soccer game."

"I want a new one!" he wails.

"I got you, little man," Cal says as they make his vanilla cone. "Can you put cookies and cream on top there? And a small empty cup too. Thanks." Cal grabs a spoon and napkin.

A moment later, he hands the cone to the boy. "Whoa! Double scoop!"

"Thank you," the dad says.

"Yeah, thank you!" the boy says.

"No problem." Cal hands the boy the spoon and napkin. "Here's how you handle a double scoop. Super-small licks, and if it starts to roll off the cone, then bam! Catch it in the cup and make the cone a hat for your new sundae." He gestures to show him what he means.

"Like a clown sundae. I had that before at Olga's."

"Awesome."

The boy pats Cal's leg, leaving a sticky handprint before walking off. Cal takes it in stride, ordering ice cream for the two of us.

A hero to a little kid? That's it. I'm done. My heart cracks open. It might not work out between us, but I'll always have a place in my heart for this man.

Of course, he doesn't need to know that. Yet.

"Your jeans are a mess," I tell him.

"Small price to pay to save the day."

We sit on the stools along the side counter. I ask him about his work. He seems to be finding his footing with his new small-town client roster. Even managing some neighborly disputes, which there are a lot of around here. The funniest is a case of a wandering cat who was taken in by a neighbor and now refuses to go back to her original owner.

"You really like it here," I say.

He smiles. "I do."

My phone vibrates with a text. Sutton: *I can't take the job. Sorry.*

I frown and show it to him.

"Shit." He pulls his phone out. "Calling her." A few moments later, he exclaims, "You're engaged? What happened? Are you pregnant?"

I gesture for him to lower his voice. He shakes his head, mouths, "Later," and heads out the door.

He stalks down the sidewalk, looking pissed. This is not good.

16

Cal

This is complete garbage. Sutton's engaged to the cheating loser who claimed he didn't want marriage. I swear he only proposed to hold her back from a job that's a great opportunity for her. She says he finally realized how much she meant to him. Right.

I slept on it, hoping to get a fresh perspective on things, and now I know what I need to do—book a flight back home. I need to see my little sister in person to talk sense into her.

After a quick shower and coffee, I sit on the sofa with my phone and search for some nonstop flights. I find one for next weekend, book it, and text Sutton that I'm coming out for a visit.

A few moments later, she texts: *You don't need to come out here. You just started a new job.*

Me: *I want to. An engagement is a big deal.*

Sutton: *Next week is Mom and Dad's anniversary. It'll be good if you're here.*

I scrub a hand over my face. I forgot about that. The days leading up to the anniversary are hard on Dad. Really, any reminder is enough to send him to a dark place. A visit is long overdue, and hopefully it'll be good for him to have both his kids home. He's become more of a recluse as he's aged. If

Sutton didn't take care of him, I'm not sure he would. That's a whole other problem.

So my weekend mission is twofold—make sure Dad takes better care of himself (or find him care) and find a tactful way of convincing Sutton not to marry John. She's too good for him.

The intercom buzzes. I wasn't expecting anyone. I go over to it. "Yeah?"

"It's Mackenzie."

Shit. She hasn't been here since our movie night during our brief fake-dating relationship. The apartment's a mess. I've been busy with work and not quite myself. I didn't bounce back like I normally do after things fizzled out between us.

I buzz her in. Then I do a quick cleanup, grabbing piles of mail, clothes, and leftover coffee mugs from around the living room. Mugs go in the kitchen.

She knocks on the door.

"Just a minute!" I pile everything else on the bedroom dresser and shut the door. Then I take my time walking to the front door, belatedly running a hand through my hair.

"Hi," she says. "Hope you don't mind me stopping by unannounced. I was wondering if Sutton's okay. She didn't tell me much about why she was turning down the job after accepting it."

"She's marrying that loser, who's determined to keep her now that she wants to leave. I'm flying out next weekend to talk sense into her."

"I'll go with you."

I stare at her blankly. "Why?"

She walks in. "I'd like to meet her in person. She's more than an assistant. We've become very friendly. Maybe I could back you up since we're friends now too." She rubs her hands together, her eyes lighting up. "What's the game plan?"

"This is a family matter. If you show up, it'll just complicate things."

"Sutton and I have a good relationship. I don't think she'd

mind meeting me. Even if she doesn't take the promotion, she'll still be our virtual assistant."

"But then you'd be meeting my dad too. Sutton still lives at home."

She settles on the sofa, so I join her. "And meeting your dad's a bad thing?"

"Dad's kind of a shut-in. He goes to work, comes home. That's it. He used to be more social, but he sorta shut down after Mom died."

"He sounds depressed."

"He probably is. He's also not the kind of guy to do anything about it."

"Would he be mad if I was there?"

"No. But he might get the wrong idea. I haven't brought a woman home since…in a long time."

Her brows draw together. I brace myself for the probing questions, but all she says is, "I'll make it clear I'm there for Sutton and you and I are just friends."

I shift forward, resting my elbows on my knees, staring at the floor. I'm not sure about Mackenzie getting involved in my family life. It's bad enough Sutton's always singing her praises. I don't want Dad to get on board. How could I possibly explain our relationship? "It's complicated" leaves so much room for questions I don't know how to answer.

"We are friends, right?" she asks, leaning down to meet my eyes. "We had ice cream together yesterday. Somebody told me that's what friends do." Her eyes sparkle playfully.

I cave. She's impossible to resist. "Okay, fine. You can go under the friendship clause."

"Ooh, a clause. How legal. So what's the plan? You do have a plan, right?"

I sit back and think for a moment. "I'm going to pull John aside and convince him this isn't what he really wants."

She grimaces. "Sutton will never forgive you for ending her relationship for her."

"You have a better idea?"

"You can talk to her about all the great potential for

growth with this job, and then I can show her stock projections with some really pretty graphs." She gestures a curve up with a finger.

I can't help my smile. I love that she likes to make graphs and play with numbers. The first day I met Hailey, she told me Mackenzie was an accounting major and graduated with honors.

"Money won't sway Sutton from the guy she thinks is the love of her life," I say.

She points at me. "Exactly, she thinks he is, but how can he be when he cheats on her and didn't propose until she was about to leave? If only there were a way to open her eyes to the cheating-loser reality."

"I'll play it by ear. You can be backup."

"Deal."

"One other thing. It might be a difficult time for Dad. It's his wedding anniversary with Mom that weekend."

"How long has it been since she died?"

I swallow over the lump in my throat. "Fifteen years."

"Does he visit her grave that day?"

"He visits her grave every Sunday. They were high school sweethearts. He's sort of lost without her." My voice comes out like a croak. Dammit. Why is it so hard to say this stuff out loud?

She hugs me. I stiffen, but she keeps her arms tight around me. Slowly, I relax, the ache easing in my throat. "I'm sorry," she says softly. "I can only imagine how hard that must be for everyone. If you think it's best I don't go—"

"You can go."

She holds my shoulders and looks into my eyes. "Sure?"

"I'm sure." Having Mackenzie at my side lightens the load. "Thank you."

Her gaze drops to my mouth. Desire stirs, but before I can reach for her, she stands, turning for the door.

"You don't have to leave," I say.

"I do." She grabs her coat and purse. "I'll see you next weekend."

"Yeah, okay."

She slips out the door. I stare blankly for a long moment, wanting to close the distance between us, with no clue how to do that.

I should ask her. If that romance novel taught me anything, it's that she's got a lot of thoughts and feelings hidden in her head. She needs some prompting to give me the secret to making things right. We have chemistry; we have friendship. Isn't that everything?

It hits me that maybe she wants me to go after her.

I push open the door and race down the stairs. When I get to the sidewalk, she's gone. She must've run, and doesn't that tell me everything I need to know?

17

Mackenzie

I missed the Clover Park spring festival this weekend to fly out to Minnesota for Sutton. It's okay, though, I did my part in the prep work, and they've got it covered for staffing. Cal dropped out of the committee after the first meeting in favor of donating money to the cause. That's one way to go.

Cal and I were on different flights, so I'm here with Sutton in the early afternoon on Friday before her dad is home from work. Her fiancé is supposed to stop by after work, so I guess then we'll have a little engagement party. She's making brownies for the occasion.

The oven timer dings. Sutton pulls the brownies from the oven and sets them on the stovetop to cool. She resembles Cal in coloring with dark brown hair and brown eyes, but her demeanor is pure sunshine whereas Cal's more serious. "Are you an end or a middle?"

"Huh?"

"Which do you like better? The crunchy end of the brownie or the gooey middle?"

"Ohhh. Both."

"I like the gooey middle. Cal likes the crunchy end. Perfect combo. He texted he's on his way."

I fidget with the end of my shirt and then smooth it out.

"Great." Things are awkward with Cal. Okay, I admit it. I'm in too deep, and I'm scared. I almost didn't take this trip, but I care about Sutton, and I want to be supportive of both her and Cal. I'm worried Cal's disapproval of her engagement will upset her.

She told me all about her fiancé, John, making him sound practically like a knight in shining armor. It's hard to believe someone as smart as Sutton could be fooled by a serial cheater. But what do I know about long-term relationships? She said they've been together since high school. Maybe knowing someone since you were an impressionable teen makes you blind to their flaws.

"Water or milk?" Sutton asks.

"Water, thanks."

She pours us glasses of water, and we take a seat in the living room with our brownies. The two-story house has furniture and decor that looks like it hasn't been updated since Cal's childhood. There's a faded green sectional sofa and a cherrywood coffee table and end tables. It's neat and tidy.

After we make short work of our brownies and Sutton fills me in on life in Minnesota, a silence falls.

"It's so nice to finally meet you in person," Sutton says for the third time since I got here.

"You too."

"If you don't mind me asking, did you come out here for me or Cal?"

I flush. "What? This has nothing to do with Cal. I just thought it was way past time that you and I met in person."

"I know he likes you."

I take a sip of water, not sure what to say.

"It's the way he says your name. He hasn't been serious about anyone since college."

"What do you mean? He lived with someone recently."

She shakes her head. "He locked up his heart after Brenda. She was his college girlfriend for a year and a half. They were pretty serious. She died in a car accident about a year after Mom died."

Poor Cal! "I had no idea."

She leans forward, her voice low, even though Cal's not here. "I probably shouldn't have said anything. I don't want you to be scared off because he's not very expressive. He's cautious. I always thought Rayna—that's the woman he lived with—was someone he chose because she understood his dedication to work. She was, too, which meant their time together was limited."

I understand cautious. After I was cheated on by the man I thought was the One (what a silly romantic notion), I shut down all other possibilities. But the grief that Cal's been through must've been tremendous. He never shared that part of his life with me. I guess I haven't talked about my past either. Fake dating doesn't exactly lead to intimacy. We enjoyed each other's company in the moment.

That's not a bad thing, right? Except part of me longs to know him better.

I notice Sutton adjusting her engagement ring like she wants me to comment on it. "So you're engaged. Congratulations!"

She beams and holds it out for me to admire. "Thank you! I'm excited. It's been a long time coming."

"Wow. And you've never dated anyone else?"

"Nope. Just one man."

"He must be special."

She turns her ring in the light, admiring the small diamond. "He is. I hope you understand why I'm not going to accept the promotion. I'm building a life here with John."

The doorbell rings. She leaps to answer it. I wipe my face for crumbs and smooth back my hair.

"Cal!" She throws her arms around him. He hugs her back and gives her ponytail a tug.

"How're you doing, beanpole?"

She beams. "You're the beanpole."

He shifts and notices me for the first time. "Hi."

"Hi."

You could cut the awkward tension with a knife. I did bolt from his apartment. I didn't know what to do. I nearly kissed him, and my track record of kissing and not hooking up with him is abysmally low. It's weird now. I don't know what to do with him and all these unrequited feelings. Does he have feelings for me buried deep down?

Sutton looks between us curiously.

"I'll get you a brownie!" Sutton carols, disappearing into the kitchen.

Cal puts a duffel bag and his coat to the side of the sofa and joins me. "Did you talk to Sutton about the job?"

"Not yet, but I'm not here to convince anyone. Just chime in with the facts. Her fiancé is stopping by after work, and I think she's hoping we can celebrate with a little engagement party. She talked about ordering takeout from a restaurant she and John like."

Sutton returns, handing him a warm brownie on a napkin.

"Thanks," Cal says. He doesn't take a bite, just stares at his little sister.

Sutton thrusts her hand out, showing off her diamond engagement ring. "I'm engaged!"

He takes her hand and examines the ring. "Kinda small."

She snatches her hand back. "It's the thought that counts."

"Is this what you really want?" Cal asks. "You've never dated anyone besides John. Isn't it possible there's another guy out there who could be a better fit? Someone who'd want you to have a great job, an education."

Sutton frowns. "There's nothing wrong with the life I want."

Cal runs a hand through his hair. "Mackenzie's offering you a great opportunity."

I jump in with my pitch. "Is it possible to have a long engagement? We'd love to have you in a bigger role. The stock options alone. Let me get my laptop, and I'll show you the projections."

Sutton shakes her head. "You really don't need to do that."

"The bonus to working with a startup," Cal says.

"Not a guarantee, but it's a definite possibility," I say, backing him up. *Team Cal!*

Sutton looks back and forth between us. "It sounds exciting, but—"

"What if you try it out?" Cal asks. "Maybe after six months to a year in Clover Park, you can move back, get married, and work remotely."

"Remote won't work for this role," I say. "But I could help John get a job in Connecticut. My family is very well connected. What does he do?" *Team Sutton!*

Sutton shakes her head. "He'll never move. He works for the family business. One day he'll be in charge. They sell and distribute rubber products."

"Oh, have they ever offered you a job there?" I ask.

"John says it's better if we don't work together."

Cal sends me an imploring look. Like I'm supposed to fix this situation. I've already made my pitch, and Sutton's so caught up in marrying John—a guy who cheats on her—she's blinded to reality. This is what's so dangerous about the love fantasy. It can derail your entire life.

On the other hand, maybe he's not as bad as Cal says. Maybe he cheated in the past when he was young and stupid, and he's seen the error of his ways. After all, Sutton's a sensible woman. She wouldn't tie herself to an unworthy guy forever. Right?

Sutton looks to me. "I really am happy. I've been dreaming of my wedding since I was a little girl."

"I'm sure you'll make a beautiful bride."

"Thanks! Cal, will you be the best man? John's not on speaking terms with his brother."

"No."

Her jaw drops. "No? But John would be happy to have you there. I'd be happy to have you there."

"I'll be at the wedding. Don't ask me to stand up for him. You know how I feel about the way he treats you."

"That was a long time ago."

Cal clamps his mouth shut. He doesn't want to be the bad guy.

Sutton huffs. "If you can't be happy for me—"

"I'm happy if you're happy," Cal says grimly.

Footsteps sound in the kitchen. "Sutton, honey, you made brownies. Thanks."

"No problem, Dad!" Sutton calls. "We've got company."

A tall man with salt-and-pepper hair walks in, holding a brownie. He looks fifties but not vibrant like my parents. He looks worn down, from his tired eyes to his slumped shoulders. "Cal, good to see you! And who's this?"

I walk over to shake his hand. "Hi, I'm Mackenzie Campbell. Sutton's been working for my company for the past year or so."

"Bill Davis." He shakes my hand firmly. He's wearing a light blue uniform shirt. Cal mentioned he works at a warehouse distribution center nearby. His brows knit together in confusion. "Are you with Cal?"

I search my brain for a polite answer. "Actually, I came to meet Sutton in person, and I confess I was hoping she'd reconsider the promotion I'm offering."

"Ah, but now she's engaged."

Cal comes over and gives his dad a half-armed hug. "How're you holding up?"

"Fine." He takes a seat in his recliner with a sigh of relief.

"I'll get you a drink," Sutton says.

"How about a beer?" Bill asks. He turns to us. "She only lets me have a beer on Fridays. I'm lucky she's letting me have sugar today too."

"Sounds like she takes good care of you," I say.

"No one asked her to," Bill grumbles.

Sutton returns with a beer for her dad. He takes it with a grateful smile. "Thanks."

"How're you really doing?" Cal asks his dad.

Bill glances at me, seeming embarrassed. "Is that why you're here? I'm doing better this year. I had a nice talk with your mom."

It's sad, but I understand keeping the connection to his deceased wife, even if he makes up her side of the conversation. I'd still want to talk to someone I loved and lost.

Cal gives a slow nod. "And what did she say?"

Bill smiles, his face lighting up. "I brought her favorite flowers, tulips. She had tulips in her bridal bouquet, you know."

"We know, Dad," Cal says gently.

Bill continues, a faraway look in his eyes, "She's waiting for me, but she wants me to be a grandparent for us first. I guess Sutton will get started on that now that she's getting married."

"I hope so," Sutton says, exchanging a sharp look with Cal that seems to say, *See? I can't leave him.*

"It's okay to miss her, Dad," Cal says. "We all do." He gestures to a photo album on the coffee table. "Looking at your wedding album again?"

Bill tears up. "Seems so unfair that someone so dedicated to helping others was taken so soon."

Cal fills me in. "Mom was an elementary school teacher and volunteered at a hospice too."

"Never thought she'd be the one in hospice," Bill says. "Ovarian cancer."

"I'm so sorry. Can I see?" I gesture toward the photo album.

Bill nods.

I flip through the album of the happy couple as bride and groom. They look like they're barely out of high school. Bill looks at his wife like he won the lottery. Cal's mom is a petite brunette, her eyes shining with happiness. "Beautiful wedding pictures. You both look so young."

Bill takes the album and gazes at his wife for a long moment before closing it. "We were. Got married a couple of years out of high school. I was playing college ball. She was working as a teacher assistant while going to night classes to become a teacher."

"You could take night classes too," Cal says to Sutton.

Sutton shakes her head. "I wasn't good at school. I couldn't wait to graduate."

"You were grieving," Bill says. "It's no wonder your grades fell. Things would be different now."

Sutton smiles, but it doesn't reach her eyes. "I'm marrying my high school sweetheart. We both have good jobs, and we'll have a nice life right here. Our kids can grow up with their grandfather like you said Mom wanted."

"Mom wants you to be happy," Bill says.

Sutton frowns and bites into a brownie.

"So tell me about you, Mackenzie," Bill says. "Sutton speaks highly of you."

"I think she's awesome too."

"Mackenzie does amazing work," Cal says.

I smile, surprised to hear him say it. "Thank you. I didn't know you knew much about my work."

"I worked with you on that conflict-of-interest case. You're smart, organized, efficient yet still know when to pass the work on to your teammates. You're a team player."

Bill lifts his brows. "High praise from Cal."

The doorbell rings.

Sutton pops up from her seat. "My fiancé is here!"

I look toward the door. John is a lanky guy in his twenties wearing a faded black T-shirt and jeans. He's scruffy looking, his light brown hair on the longish side with an unkempt beard. His eyes shift around the room warily. If ever a man looked guilty, it's this one. You would think he'd feel perfectly comfortable with Sutton's family after eight years.

"What's going on?" he asks.

Sutton walks to his side. "Remember I told you Cal's stopping by for a visit, and Mackenzie's my boss at Brooks Campbell Security. I told them we should get takeout and have a little engagement party. Oh! Mackenzie, this is John, my fiancé."

"Nice to meet you," I say.

He lifts a hand. "You too. Cal."

"John," Cal says flatly.

Bill sips his beer and says nothing.

"Would you like a brownie?" Sutton asks John cheerfully, smoothing over the tension.

"Nah, I had something before I got here."

Sutton gestures toward the sofa. "Come and sit. I'll get you a beer."

John perches on the arm of the sofa near where Sutton was sitting. Sutton hurries into the kitchen. He didn't even thank Sutton for getting him a beer.

"Congratulations on your engagement," I say to John.

"That's what she wanted," John says. "It was that or she walks."

"Maybe she should've walked," Cal says under his breath.

Bill jumps in. "John, how's your dad?"

"Same old, same old."

The doorbell rings. Bill looks over. "Now who could that be?"

Sutton returns and hands John his beer. He still doesn't thank her. Just pops the top and takes a long swallow.

Cal opens the door to a woman with brown curly hair in a messy ponytail. Her face is tear-streaked with mascara, and she's wearing a long sweater over her very pregnant belly.

18

John leaps to his feet, spilling his beer. "Shit."

"You must be Sutton," the pregnant woman says, focusing on her. She looks around the room. "Or is it you?" She jabs a finger at me.

I shake my head.

Sutton stands. "I'm Sutton. Who are you?"

"Olivia. Please don't marry my baby daddy. He only proposed because you were going to leave, but me and the baby need him more."

Sutton's eyes widen, her jaw dropping.

"She's crazy!" John says. "Don't listen to her."

"We've been seeing each other for two years," Olivia says. "And we were happy until this whole proposal thing."

"Proposal thing," Sutton echoes softly before swaying on her feet. Cal puts a protective arm around her, anchoring her to his side.

"Olivia, you need to go," Cal says firmly. "You too, John. Seems like you two have a lot to talk about."

When John doesn't move fast enough, Bill grabs him by the arm and escorts him to the door.

"Don't come back," Bill says, pushing him out the door. He shuts the door behind them and locks it.

Sutton's lower lip wobbles. Cal goes to hug her, but she shakes her head, pulling off her engagement ring.

She unlocks the door and throws it at John. "Screw you!"

I watch through the large front window as John scrambles to pick the ring up off the grass and offers it to Olivia. Amazingly, she accepts the ring, and they leave with their arms around each other.

Sutton slams the door and puts her hands to her temples. "Stupid, stupid, stupid!" Her voice rises to an ear-splitting register.

"He's stupid not you," Cal says.

Tears slide down Sutton's cheeks, and she wipes them away angrily.

"I'm so sorry," I say.

Bill crosses his arms. "I never liked him."

"Dad!" Sutton exclaims. "Why didn't you say anything?"

"I know better than to get between a couple. Why do you think your mom stopped talking to her parents?"

"What do you mean?" Cal asks.

"She said they moved away," Sutton says.

Bill takes a seat, gesturing for us to follow. Then he shares a story about his wife's parents' disapproval of them and how nothing he did could change their minds. They wanted her to marry a guy who would take over their dairy farm. That wasn't him. "I was a good architect until I couldn't focus anymore. Once you lose your heart, it's hard to find meaning in a job."

"That's called grief," Cal says. "You could still go back to being an architect."

"It's been fifteen years since I did that. So much has changed. No, that part of my life's over."

Cal exhales sharply, resting his elbows on his knees. It hits me that Cal's afraid to love. He lost someone close to him not once but twice at a time when he really needed someone in his life. He was young, eighteen, nineteen. And his dad must've been no help. Even now, his dad's just surviving. Oh God, I want to help, but I don't know what to do.

I want to help Cal to love again, to love me. And I want to help Bill and Sutton too. But I can't fix this family, and it's not my place to do so. What will happen to Bill if Sutton moves more than a thousand miles away? On the other hand, is Sutton obligated to take care of her father for the rest of his life? He's a healthy man in his fifties.

Will Sutton do okay with such a big change in her life? Will Cal ever let love in again? My mind is spinning, my heart aching. The only thing I can think to do is be a good boss.

"Do you want some time off, Sutton?" I ask. "Given the circumstances."

Sutton lifts her chin. "I've wasted too much time on John as it is. I'm going to take that job." She turns to her dad. "If it's okay with you."

"It's okay with me." He looks toward the ceiling for a long moment before meeting Sutton's eyes. "Mom's okay with it too."

Sutton blinks back tears. "Thanks."

My throat chokes with emotion. The great love he must've lost. He's still living with a ghost to find comfort. It's at once beautiful and heartbreaking.

"You can stay with me for a while," Cal says to Sutton. "I'll take the couch."

"You're welcome to stay with me too," I say. "We have a couple of spare bedrooms. I share a house with my cousin Harper."

Sutton gives me a watery smile. Cal jumps up, grabs a tissue, and hands it to her. "I'll stay with Cal, but thanks."

Cal sits on the edge of the sofa and puts an arm around his sister. "You can stay with me as long as you need to. I'll help you pack. We'll video chat with Dad every week. Okay, Dad?"

Bill keeps a stiff upper lip and nods once. His eyes are red.

Sutton rests her head against Cal's side and sighs. He kisses the top of her head and gives me a relieved look. I wish I could hug them all.

~

Cal

I changed my flight to Monday so I could fly back with Sutton. Mackenzie did too. That gave us the whole weekend with Dad. Mackenzie jumped right in with my family, supportive and just the right amount of sympathetic with Sutton. She even organized Dad's kitchen and made meal planning easy with ready-made grocery lists. But the topper —she baked apple pie for him. I had no idea she could make pie from scratch. He's in love.

As I dig into my slice of pie, sitting across the table from Dad, I'm starting to think I'm in love with her too. My heart jumps at the thought, but the usual panic feeling doesn't follow. The sound of female laughter reaches us from the living room. Mackenzie's a miracle worker. Getting a laugh out of Sutton the day after her eight-year relationship ends is not something I could pull off.

Dad points his fork at me. "This is the best pie I've ever tasted. Hang onto that one."

"Sure, that's a good reason to be with someone. Pie."

"I've seen the way you look at her. And I can't imagine she'd come all this way, taking care of all of us, if she didn't feel the same way."

"She came for Sutton."

"Come on, Cal."

"It's complicated." That's what Mackenzie said about us when we were fake dating. I don't know what we are now, but complicated about sums it up.

Dad takes my pie from me.

"Hey!"

"You get this back when you get your head on straight."

"What? I suck at relationships."

"Or maybe you're afraid you'll get hurt, so you blow them up before they can go anywhere."

"No, that's not it." *Is it?* I reach for my pie, and he takes a bite of it. Dammit.

"You don't deserve her pie."

I throw my palms up. "What do you want me to do, be like you? Marry someone, make them the center of my universe, and then lose everything?"

"I didn't lose everything. Mom's still with me. She's here with you too, watching from above."

I drop my head in my hands. I'm glad it makes him feel better to believe it, but I just can't. She's gone, and he has to live the rest of his life without her. He's never been able to move on or let go. He hasn't even donated her clothes. They're all in the dresser and closet exactly as she left them. Her muddy shoes are still by the back door.

I have nothing left from Brenda. Her parents took it all. I had to delete the pictures from my phone. They only caused more pain. This is why I keep the pain in a box because otherwise I'll be like Dad with no life whatsoever.

"Mom wants you to be happy."

I lift my head, suddenly exhausted. "Dad, you lost your career. You only leave the house for work. You never do anything or visit anyone."

"I have all I need right here."

"Sutton is leaving. It'll be just you here. What're you going to do when you retire? Sit home by yourself all the time?"

His chin juts out. "I'll do whatever I want. If I want to stay home, that's my right."

I let out a breath. "I don't want to fight. You live your life, and I'll live mine." I get up and get another slice of pie for myself. I'm not going to fight him over my pie.

"Cal, love is worth it."

I stand by the counter and shovel pie in my mouth.

"You can't let fear hold you back," he says.

I swallow the pie that's suddenly like concrete going down my throat. "Dad, when I look at you and what you've lost, all I see is a cautionary tale."

"A cautionary tale!"

I set down my fork. "You've been depressed for fifteen years."

"But I was happy for twenty-six years. I'll take that any day. I want you to have someone special in your life."

I shake my head. "Maybe I'll get a dog."

"A dog is no substitute for a wife."

"Oh my God," Sutton says from behind us. "You're embarrassing yourselves and me."

Mackenzie gives me a cheeky smile. "You'd need a cat for a wife substitute. Make that nine. You can be the crazy cat man."

Dad laughs. My ears burn hot, though she doesn't seem in the least offended. Maybe having brothers made her immune to insults.

"I sure do love this pie, Mackenzie," Dad says, a hint of worship in his eyes.

Mackenzie pulls out her phone. "What's your number? I'll text you the recipe. Then you can make it whenever you want."

"Oh, I wouldn't know how to bake anything like that."

"That's what recipes are for. And you know what? Even the baking fails are tasty."

She pulls out a chair and texts him while talking to him about easy dinner recipes and her favorite cooking shows. By the time she's done, Dad's agreed to start cooking for himself and trying a baked recipe on the weekends.

Is there anything this woman can't do?

I spend the rest of the weekend marveling over Mackenzie's ease with Dad and Sutton, even me. She's surprisingly domestic while also being take-charge and organized. She's a whirlwind of power and love. I don't think I've ever met another woman like her. She really is the best person I've ever met. Maybe I should tell her that when she's awake.

On the flight home, Mackenzie falls asleep on my shoulder. Sutton's on my other side, watching a movie. I smooth

Mackenzie's hair back, tempted to kiss her on the head. Could I see myself with her in the long run?

I tense. What if...I push the dark fear down. If I don't think about it, it doesn't exist. Fear stops me. I want the opposite—

Hope.

But after we land and get our luggage, Mackenzie says, "I'm in long-term parking. Sutton, I'll see you tomorrow at work. Cal, I'll see you at the vow-renewal ceremony next weekend. If it's okay with you, I'll tell Mom our fake relationship ended after the ceremony. I don't want any weirdness on their special day."

My throat catches, and I clear it. "Right." Why was I thinking there was more between us? I feel like a fool. Dad's talk put all kinds of crazy ideas in my head.

Sutton wrinkles her nose. "Fake relationship?"

"Long story," I say, holding Mackenzie's gaze. She doesn't blink.

"About to be resolved soon," Mackenzie says. She turns to Sutton. "When you meet my mom, you'll understand."

"No one would believe you were faking it," Sutton says.

I study Mackenzie. Maybe she wasn't faking it?

"Good!" Mackenzie says brightly. "We've done our job." She hugs Sutton and gives me a short wave before striding away, pulling her wheeled suitcase behind her.

"Who's having a vow-renewal ceremony?" Sutton asks me.

"Her parents."

"Sounds romantic. Good time for you to make your move."

"Let's go find your luggage."

19

The vow-renewal ceremony at Ludbury House looks like a wedding to me. In the two-story foyer of the mansion, friends and family gather to watch Hailey descend the grand staircase toward her husband, Josh. A short veil is perched on her head, paired with a white silk dress that ends at the knees. Flowers everywhere, classical music piped in, even a minister to perform the ceremony.

There's a few rows of chairs with white satin covers. The rest is standing room only. I stand in the back. Mackenzie and her brothers, Cooper and Finn, are in the front row, along with the grandparents and Rowan.

The minister prompts Hailey to give her vow. She does so without any notes, her eyes shiny with tears, her voice strong. "Josh, I'd marry you all over again. You are my rock. You've shown me what love truly is, and I vow to spend the rest of my life loving you through good times and bad, sickness and health. You are truly my warrior beast."

People laugh, but I can't manage it over the lump in my throat. I don't even know what a warrior beast is. The emotion in her voice gets to me.

Josh cups her cheek, wiping a tear with his thumb. She does the same for him. He kisses her cheek.

He exhales sharply. "Hard to top that. I call you warrior

princess because you're fierce. Strong, tough, but also loving and so beautiful. I don't know how I got so lucky." His voice breaks.

My eyes water. I catch Mackenzie wiping her eyes.

Josh continues, "I vow to love and protect you for the rest of my life. You are my heart. That's it. You are my heart."

Hailey cups his face, and he leans into her hand. The love is so real, so strong I can feel it all the way back here. I can't breathe. I need air, the room suddenly too hot. The minister goes on with the ceremony.

I escape out the front door, my head spinning. I sit on the porch and put my head between my knees. What is wrong with me? I force myself to take slow, deep breaths.

After a few moments, I straighten, staring out at the church across the street. I've been to weddings before, seen vows before. I've never heard so much emotion, witnessed so much love. It must be terrifying to love someone like that. How can they bear it? Don't they know they could lose everything?

∽

Mackenzie

I glance around the ballroom, looking for Cal. The reception is just getting started with cocktails and appetizers. I saw him before the ceremony, and he disappeared. Did he walk out in the middle of the ceremony? Is he coming back? I guess I can make up an excuse that he wasn't feeling well. As far as my family's concerned, Cal and I are still a couple. It's definitely time to end the game. Would it be possible to try this for real?

My breath catches as Cal strides in, heading straight for me, looking intimidatingly serious. "Cal? Is everything okay?"

"No."

Mom appears by my side. "Wasn't it a beautiful ceremony? I'm so glad to have it here. Our wedding was in Villroy, and part of me always wished I could have a second wedding here, and now I have."

"It was beautiful, Mom."

"Very nice," Cal says. His voice sounds hoarse.

Mom beams. "Maybe we'll be planning something for you two at Ludbury House soon."

I frown. "Let's not go there, Mom."

"So you're not serious?" Mom asks, blinking innocently.

I look over her shoulder. "Oh look, Aunt Charlotte is signaling you. I bet your friends have a special gift waiting for you."

"That would be just like them!" Mom chirps and hurries off to meet up with her friends. Chances are they do have a special gift for her. It's sort of their thing on big occasions.

"Can we step outside to talk?" Cal asks.

My brows draw together, nerves skittering through me. Cal has never asked to talk. Not once. "Sure." I lead the way through the front hall to the door.

As soon as we step onto the front porch, Cal barks, "This fake relationship was a huge mistake! Your mom's dropping hints about wedding planning. It's not right to trick her."

I grip my hands together. He can't even think about the idea of being with me long-term without panicking. "She only dropped a hint because that's her job. Letting people know she'll plan their weddings. No need to panic."

He starts pacing. "I don't know whether I'm coming or going with you. It's like we're together, we're pretending we're together, then we're just friends, then you're bonding with my family. What is that? What are we doing?" He stops pacing and looks at me expectantly.

I cross my arms, hugging myself. "I-I don't know. I just wanted to help you and Sutton any way I can, and…I don't know."

He pushes a hand through his hair, rumpling it. "I don't know either."

"Okay."

We stare at each other for a long moment. My legs feel

shaky, the awful point of no return approaching. I can feel it. I don't know where we go from here. My heart races even as time slows down.

He takes a deep breath. "We need to stop seeing each other. Fake, friends, or otherwise."

My gut clenches. It hurts more than expected to hear him say it.

I lift my chin, determined not to cry in front of him. "Okay, then. I think you should go now."

"I should say goodbye to your parents."

I shake my head. "I'll say goodbye for you."

He stands there, studying me like he's trying to figure me out. What does he expect me to say after he ended things?

"Goodbye, Mackenzie." He turns and strides down the steps.

"Bye," I manage through the knot in my throat.

I slink back inside and rush into the bathroom for a good cry. Damn him for expecting me to explain our relationship. It's not like I planned to fall in love with him and hope he'd join me, which he didn't. I drop my head in my hands. This whole thing is so *exhausting*.

After a few calming breaths, I splash cold water on my face. I take one step out of the bathroom and come face-to-face with Mom. She takes in my cry face, puts an arm around my shoulders, and guides me into her office, shutting the door behind us.

I take a seat in her cushy desk chair, and she pulls her other chair next to me. "Is it Cal?" she asks.

"We broke up."

"Oh, honey, I'm so sorry. I know that hurts."

A spark of anger flares. I wouldn't be in this mess if she hadn't been matchmaking my entire adult life. "It didn't help that you hinted about planning our wedding."

She hands me a tissue. "It couldn't have been a strong relationship if a hint can destroy it. You're better off."

I dab at the tears with the tissue, torn between anger and grief. "Everything backfired." My voice chokes. "I had all these inconvenient feelings, and then I messed it up, and he acted all weird, and now I'm getting dumped when I should've been the one walking away."

"Mackenzie, sweetheart, you have inconvenient feelings? That's wonderful!"

"That's all you got from that?"

"It's the first time you've had deep feelings. That *is* wonderful."

I glare at her as best I can with swollen cry eyes. "No, it's not wonderful because those feelings are not returned, and I'm the idiot who kept getting in deeper."

She rubs my back.

"The whole thing was supposed to be fake!" I cry in despair. "And I said no sex because boundaries, but then there was kissing and, oh, this is all your fault. I thought you were secretly matchmaking when you told me to stay away from him, so I pretended we were a couple to catch you in the act."

I glance up, feeling stupid.

Mom gives me a small smile. "Hmm. Well, I was of two minds when it came to Cal. I really like him as a person, but I was wary because of the live-in girlfriend situation. She clearly thought marriage was right around the corner. That to me says mismatched expectations, which could've been down to better communication, or it could mean he's anti-marriage."

I sniffle. "So you weren't using reverse psychology to get me to be with him?"

"Have I ever used reverse psychology on you?"

I think about that. Besides the matchmaking, she's always been straightforward with me. Well, not completely. "You always said the door was open for me to join as a partner in your business, and then you chose Rowan as partner."

Her pale blue eyes widen. "But you never wanted that. You have your own business."

"That's where the reverse psychology comes in. Now that

I'm closed out of it, I want the option. Maybe that was your plan."

She huffs. "I'm not sure where you got the idea that I was manipulative. All I've ever wanted is your happiness. I love you unconditionally. I'm so proud of the woman you've become and the way you've forged your own way in the world. If you really want to join me in my business, that door is still open. Maybe one day you and Rowan can run it together."

That's exactly what Cal said. I burst into tears.

She pulls me close, smoothing my hair like she did when I was little. "Oh, honey."

I sob into her perfect white dress. "I could never live up to your beauty-queen standards. I could never follow in your high heels."

She leans back, cupping my face. "My darling daughter, you were never meant to. Dad and I wanted you to be a leader not a follower. We wanted you to be strong and confident, and you are."

I grab a tissue and try to dry her dress. She waves me away. "Don't worry about it. You're more important."

My lower lip quivers. "Being a strong woman with a blackbelt isn't the same as being like you."

"What is it about me you want to be like?"

My throat clogs with emotion, my inner little girl finally finding her voice. "I want to be beautiful and successful like you."

She strokes my hair back from my face. "You are."

"I want to be good at business like you, a master networker."

She sighs. "That didn't happen overnight. You're well on your way. Now you have four full-time employees. That's more than I ever had. And you don't have to work weekends. Smart move."

I laugh a little, but it turns into a sob. "I don't think I'll ever find the One."

"You always said you didn't believe in the One."

"That's because I thought it was vanishingly rare. Not something I could ever expect, and then Cal made me hope." My voice breaks.

"Sometimes the One is right under our nose, but we don't see it for a while."

"That was true for you and Dad. Not me and Cal."

"Okay," she says indulgently.

I give her a hard stare. "Do you swear you weren't doing any matchmaking between me and Cal?"

She cocks her head. "Oh, what was that? I think Rowan's saying it's time for cake. We'd better go over there."

"I knew it!" I look to the ceiling, relief flooding me. I'm not crazy or paranoid. She was totally matchmaking me! No wonder I resorted to fake dating. "All that networking to help Cal was to see how he'd fit in with our family."

"And to help him. It's not easy to build a client list. If he didn't have enough work, he might not have stuck around."

I hold up a finger. "Promise you won't interfere with Finn." My younger brother deserves to skip all this drama.

She smiles. "I don't have to. He's kept in touch with Olivia all on his own. She's the One for him."

"Doubtful. They live on opposite coasts, she's four years older than him, and they're on completely different career paths."

"Time will tell. Come on, let's go have cake."

I go with her and watch my parents slice the cake and feed it to each other playfully. Bittersweet. I'm so happy for them and so sad for me. Why didn't I stick with my gut where Cal was concerned? I ended it early on before any heavy emotions moved in to lodge in my heart. That was the right move. The rest was a mistake.

The next morning I drag myself out of bed and force myself to go running. After a night of too much crying, I could use the endorphins.

Just as I'm dragging myself home, I see Sutton jogging toward me. "I didn't know you were a runner too."

She smiles. "It's new. I have a lot of rage. Wasted years, betrayal, regret, the whole sandwich."

"You mean the whole enchilada?"

"Exactly. Did you and Cal get in a fight? He's upset, and you look like you lost your best friend. And I get it. I feel like I lost my best friend, even though he turned out to be a weasel."

"Do you want to come in? I live up there." I point toward my house.

"I'd love some girl time."

"Me too. My cousin Harper should be home soon too. You'll like her. She tells it like it is, though I have to warn you she thinks she's funny. Not so much."

She laughs a little. "Okay."

A short while later, we settle at the kitchen table with tea and chocolate chip cookies. Yes, I've been stress baking. "Harper will be home in about an hour."

Sutton warms her hands on the mug. "I can't wait to start work on Monday. I could use the distraction."

"If you want, you can get familiar with this organizational software I'm trying out. It's a work scheduling app I'm hoping will make it easier for the team to stay on the same page. I'll show you."

"Sure."

We spend the next hour talking about the program as we snarf down cookies. I'm high on sugar when Harper gets home.

"Mmm, cookies." She smiles and walks over to Sutton. "Hi! I'm Harper."

"I'm Sutton, the new office manager for Brooks Campbell Security."

Harper narrows her eyes at the laptop. "Don't tell me Mackenzie's making you work on the weekend."

"I asked her to. I'm getting over a breakup and need the distraction."

"Same here," I say. "My fake relationship is over."

Harper takes a cookie. "Did you fake break up?"

I get teary.

She pulls out a seat. "Oh no, what happened? Did it get too real?" I guess I didn't tell Harper the whole story. All these feelings I didn't want to admit to anyone. For good reason too. Now they left a hole in my heart.

I nod. "I'm an idiot. I knew I should've kept it casual from the start. He came at me demanding answers for how complicated things got, and then when I said I don't know the answer, he ended it. Fake, friends, or otherwise, his exact words. It takes two people to make a complication, right?"

"Right," Harper says around a bite of cookie. "What a jerk."

"Hey! That's my brother," Sutton says. "He seems upset too."

"Sorry," Harper says. "Usually in solidarity we follow the all-men-are-pigs rule."

Sutton laughs. "Let me tell you about my pig." She fills Harper in on the John situation, complete with the pregnant girlfriend.

"Damn," Harper says. "You win the loser Olympics. Not you, him. You deserve all the cookies and the wine too."

"It's not even noon," I say.

"At least give her milk. Sutton, you can dunk as much as you want, and we won't make any comments about gross crumbs."

Sutton laughs. "You said she was funny."

Harper leans back and smirks. "See, Sutton thinks I'm funny."

I roll my eyes. "I said 'she thinks she's funny,' meaning you think that. Not you are funny."

"Hmph. Milk?"

"Yes, please," Sutton says.

Harper gets out the milk and pours Sutton a glass. "Did Cal say why he wanted to end the fake-dating thing? Maybe he wants the real thing?"

"Oh!" Sutton exclaims. "That could be it. When we were at Dad's house, Cal kept watching you with this adoring puppy-dog look when he thought you weren't looking."

"Doubtful," I say. "I have to move on. My heart can't take this back and forth anymore. Sutton, if you want a running partner, I run every morning at six a.m. Unless I've had a late night. Sleep's just as important as exercise, and it really helps with stress like from certain unmentionable people."

Sutton dunks her cookie in milk and takes a bite, her expression blissful. Fresh-baked cookies can do that for a person. "Sure. Can we do seven?"

"That works too." I sigh, wishing I could bounce back the way Sutton seems to be doing. She's one of those naturally cheerful people. Cal said she was like sunshine. Cal with the dark soulful eyes, the terrible taste in baseball movies, the sexy everything, the tolerance for my family. You don't find that combination in just anyone. This sucks. I wish—

"Okay, I'm only going to say this once," Harper announces, startling me out of my downward spiral. "I saw you after you first hooked up with Cal, and you were smitten."

"Smitten?" I echo, shocked she'd use a word like that. Then I remember she's shifted to the dark side. She's a romance reader who *believes*.

"Aww," Sutton says. "I could totally see that the first time I saw you two together on our video call."

I purse my lips. "I was not smitten. I've never been smitten in my life."

Harper barrels on. "You couldn't stay away from him, and even after you ended it, you still found a way to spend time with him with your whole fake-relationship thing."

Sutton shakes her head. "You guys didn't look like you were faking at my dad's house."

"That was us being friends at that point," I say.

Sutton tilts her head. "I didn't get that feeling at all."

"Nobody did," Harper says. "So let's review. You introduced yourself to him as someone not looking for anything serious. You were upfront with strong boundaries."

"Yes!" Finally they're understanding why this is all Cal's fault.

"Now it's time to let him know you're serious about him," Harper says. "Things changed. Feelings happened."

I open my mouth and promptly shut it.

"On both sides," Sutton says. "I could totally tell. He's not good at showing it, but he cares deeply. I'm talking love territory."

My heart pounds.

Harper takes a sip of my tea and makes a face. Probably because it's cold. "Be as direct about your feelings as you were about your boundaries and you'll be fine."

"But I'm not sure he returns those feelings." He was in a panic after the vow renewal and Mom's hint about our future wedding. It doesn't exactly scream I have vulnerable feelings for you. Is it possible they're buried deep down? Is he as scared of taking a chance on me as I am with him?

"I'm sure," Sutton says. "I'm telling you, when you weren't looking, he had an adoring-puppy look. That's the Cal version of love."

My lips quirk to the side. Sutton reads too many romance novels.

Harper hands me a cookie. "I think he's feeling something deep too. No guy sends flowers after a one-night stand they don't plan to see again."

"He sent flowers?" Sutton asks on a sigh. "Flowers are so nice. John said flowers are a waste of money."

Harper shakes her head. "Girl, what were you thinking with that one?"

Sutton traces a circle on the table. "He was my high school sweetheart. I thought we'd have a lifelong love like my parents. Well, before Mom died."

"Seems like their love continues still," I say gently.

Sutton nods. "Yeah. I guess that's not my path after all."

"Everyone's path is different. Right?" Harper says. "My

parents met by accident when my dad and Mackenzie's dad switched places on a date. Our dads are identical twins."

Sutton brightens. "Ooh! I'd love to hear that story. A twin switcheroo!"

I stand abruptly and nearly trip over Felix. My cat manages to always be underfoot when I least expect it. "I have to go buy some flowers."

"Go get 'em!" Harper cheers.

Sutton gives me a thumbs-up.

I rush from the room before I can lose my nerve.

Cal

I get home from a long walk to find Mackenzie sitting on my front porch, holding a bouquet of white roses. "What're you doing here?" My voice sounds harsher than I mean to because I'm shocked. I pushed her away so hard, and she's here with flowers. No one's ever given me flowers before.

"Giving you these," she says, handing me the roses. "White roses are for new beginnings."

I take them from her, unsure what she means.

She gives me an uncertain smile. "There's a card."

I pull the card from the small envelope and read: Can we start over?

I stare at her, speechless. A sliver of hope pokes in, prodding me to talk to her. See where this goes. "Come in."

I lead the way into my apartment. A few moments later we're on the sofa. She tucks a leg underneath her. I realize I'm still holding the roses and set them on the coffee table. I don't have a vase. Never needed one.

"Sutton says you're in love with me," she says.

I suck in air. Dammit. I never said that.

Am I in love with her?

She looks at me, vulnerability in her blue eyes. It was brave of her to say that. Still I hesitate, wary she'll expect something big like my entire life. The price you pay for love.

She rushes on. "I'd like a fresh start. I introduced myself to you as someone who only wanted casual, but that was before I met you." She blinks rapidly like she's about to cry. Instinctively I reach for her hand to comfort her.

She pulls away. "It's easier if we don't touch. It kinda messes with my head."

"Okay."

"Because of our chemistry."

"Oh." *That's good.* "I'm sorry about the way I ended things. I guess I got overwhelmed at all the—" I cough "—emotion flying around at the vow renewal. I know that sounds weird."

"Not at all! I have emotions too. I mean about you." She buries her face in her hands and mumbles, "Why is this so hard?" She lifts her head and meets my eyes dead on. "I have feelings for you. Deep feelings. I'm scared, but there it is."

I shift closer. "You're scared? I can't imagine you being scared of anything."

"Ha! I'm terrified. I didn't want to fall in love with you. It's messy and painful, and I'm terrified it won't work out, and I'll suffer *terribly*."

My shoulders relax. No one's ever acknowledged the suffering connected to loving someone. "I get that. I never believed that saying about better to have loved and lost than never to have loved at all. Grief can steal your life."

"Sutton told me about Brenda. Have you ever gone to grief counseling?"

I close my eyes. Sutton had no right to share that. I hate talking about it.

"Would you consider counseling?" she asks. "I sense your pain. I understand how hard it is to let someone in after what you've been through."

I stare straight ahead, keeping my voice steady. "If I open that box, the one I push the pain into, I won't be me anymore. I won't function."

She slides her hand to the nape of my neck and presses her forehead to mine. "Oh, Cal. You will function, I promise.

Pushing the pain away never makes it leave completely. Then you're stuck with only the pain and not the good memories."

I slide my hand into her hair and breathe with her, calm returning. "I don't want to end up like him." I shift back to look at her. "I want the good part, but not the rest."

She blinks back tears. "I don't think love works like that. Life doesn't work like that, I know that for sure." She pulls away. "That is, if you feel the same way about me."

It hits me that I fell the moment I took her in my arms on the dance floor the first day we met. Why was I fighting it so long? Every time things got too intense, I put up a wall. "I never believed in love at first sight."

"Me either. That's silly."

"Until you."

"Oh, Cal." She loops her arms around my neck. I kiss her, putting all the love and longing I've tried to hold back into the single moment.

I cradle her face in my hands and push past every wall to say what's in my heart. "I love you, Mackenzie."

She lets out a small cry, smiling with watery eyes. "I love you too. Let's end this game between us. No more back and forth, running scared. I'm all in." She laughs and holds up a shaking hand. "This is me with my heart on the line."

I take her shaking hand in mine and kiss it. Somehow her vulnerability makes it easier for me to bear mine. It's hard to speak around the lump of emotion lodged in my throat. "I'll take good care of you."

She smiles. "We'll take care of each other."

I swallow hard. "You're pretty healthy, right? Your family seem healthy."

"We're a hardy bunch. And so are you."

My mouth goes dry, my voice not entirely steady. "Okay." This is harder than I thought, facing fears of death. It's all wrapped up with love for me. No wonder I've avoided it for so long.

She climbs into my lap, her eyes intent on mine. "You will never, ever lose me. Even if I die first, you'll still have me here." She touches my head. "And here." She touches my heart. "We love each other, and that's a good thing. We can be very happy together, I know it. All I'm asking is for you to open your heart and let me in."

My eyes sting. "You're already there."

She kisses me, and I return it, losing myself in sensation. Nothing has ever felt so right. She lifts her head. "I'm ready for makeup sex. Take me to the bedroom."

I stand, cradling her in my arms. I can't say no to this woman. Never could right from the start. And I'm better off for it. "So bossy."

She kisses my jaw. "So are you in exactly the way I like— in the bedroom."

"I love you." The words come a little easier now.

"I love you too."

My throat tightens. This love stuff takes a lot out of you.

I set her gently on the bed and lower myself over her, gazing into her shining eyes.

And love gives back everything.

EPILOGUE

Six months later...

Mackenzie

It's our housewarming party! Except I already live here. Cal moved into my house and paid Harper her share of the equity in it. My man is a big-time saver. The accountant in me finds that so sexy. Ha.

My parents are here, along with my brothers, Cooper and Finn; Cooper's wife, Rowan; and Harper, of course. My cousin Owen's off with Shayla on location in LA for a month, working on finding more clients while she does some post-production scenes for a movie. Nathan's here, Sutton, and the newlywed Mason and May with their daughter, Sophie. More people are on their way.

I put on my house-party playlist, starting with Flo Rida's "My House." Harper catches my eye, and we immediately shift in unison to raise the roof, palms up. We'll move on to a few jumping moves and then spin on a certain beat. Yes, we have a kitchen dance routine, only now we're in the living room.

Felix, my antisocial cat, wraps himself around Sutton's leg. He used to only be attached to me, then Rowan, and now

Sutton. I think he senses when someone needs him, though Sutton seems to be doing much better now after her terrible breakup six months ago. She's even going to do a sologamy ceremony with me, Harper, Rowan, and Shayla. We're waiting for Shayla to wrap things up in LA.

Cal joins me and Harper in raising the roof. He looks ridiculous, which tells me I probably do too. I pull his hands down and start dancing with him. Harper continues the routine on her own.

"Good turnout for a housewarming party," he says loudly over the music.

"I know, right?"

"Especially considering you already live here."

I grin. "My family uses any excuse to get together and celebrate."

"Too bad I couldn't get Dad out here."

"Maybe he can drive over with Henry for the holidays." His dad recently adopted a standard poodle, all black, named Henry. The dog has been such a blessing for him, the perfect emotional support animal. Bill's started to meet more people, taking Henry on walks and to the dog park. He won't leave the dog for more than a day, although now that Cal and Sutton both live in Clover Park, he's been talking about relocating.

Sutton joins us, holding Felix in her arms. He tucks his head into her neck, closing his eyes. "Happy housewarming!"

"Thanks. You seem as happy as we are," I say.

"She's happy to finally have my apartment to herself," Cal says. He moved in with me last month. It was important to him to spend some time in grief counseling before taking the next step with me. I supported him in that one hundred percent. Sutton even joined him for a few sessions. He seems lighter now, not so serious. Like the weight he'd been carrying for more than a decade finally lifted.

Sutton inclines her head. "He's a slob. You'll see."

"I am not," Cal says.

"Have you seen the way he leaves the potholders on the counter? And he never hangs up the dishtowel." She shakes her head. "They have a place, Cal."

Sutton, it turns out, is a neat freak. I've actually found Cal to be fairly organized. His clothes make it into the hamper, he cleans the sink after he trims his beard, and, most importantly, the toilet seat is always down.

I defend Cal's honor. "I find him to be a considerate and neat roommate."

"I'm a little more than that." Cal grabs me and nips my neck.

I squeal and slap at his shoulder. "Back off, vampire."

He grins. Sutton shakes her head, smiling.

Cal and I mingle as more family and friends show up. Even my cousin Rafael is here from the city. He's Owen and Harper's younger brother. He's got his digital camera at the ready, snapping pics. So nice of him to do that for us. He's a professional photographer, mostly doing shoots for models.

I give Rafael a hug. Like me, he has brown hair and blue eyes, tall with a mix of his parents' looks. His dad's sharp jaw, his mom's full lips. His easy smile earns him friends and lots of admirers. "Thanks for coming, Rafael! It's so great to see you."

"You too." He shakes Cal's hand. "Congrats!"

"On living together, thanks," Cal says, which is kinda strange. I thought Rafael was congratulating us on being a couple.

I put a hand on Rafael's arm. "You don't have to take pictures the whole time. Just relax."

"I don't mind." His head swivels as he spots Sutton. "Who is that?"

"My baby sister," Cal says with a hint of a growl.

Rafael can't take his eyes off her. "She's beautiful. I wonder if she'd mind if I took her picture."

"Only one way to find out," I say.

Rafael heads over to her. And on that note, I pull Cal

away. Sutton is a grown-ass woman who doesn't need her big brother running interference. "Let's get the champagne."

Cal follows me to the kitchen. "Can we trust him? Sutton just came out of a long-term relationship."

"That was six months ago. You came out of a serious relationship the same day I snatched you up." I grin.

He doesn't smile. "Seriously."

"Of course you can trust him! He's my cousin. Also, he's a model photographer surrounded by beautiful women at work, and they find him in the wild too. He was probably artistically inspired."

He grunts. "Not making me feel much better."

I kiss him, lingering a little longer than is decent at a party. He gives me a tender smile and laces his fingers with mine. I continue our journey to the kitchen, pleased with how easy it is to distract him. It takes a while to get to the kitchen because more people keep arriving and stopping us to chat.

Once we're finally alone in the kitchen, he boxes me in against the counter and kisses me, long and deep. By the time he pulls away, I'm dizzy with lust. He gazes into my eyes with so much love I'm momentarily speechless. I love him so damn much.

He cups my face in his hands, his voice husky. "I knew the moment I set eyes on you at that Valentine's Day dance my world would never be the same."

My throat tightens. "Oh, Cal. You're so sweet."

"I know all you saw was a sexy guy you had to have."

I laugh. It's his favorite story, how I saw green flags with his commitment-phobe self and a fabulous way to end my dry spell. "And I got so much more."

He strokes my cheek with his thumb. "I love you."

"I love you too."

"I know we've only been living together for a month, but it feels right. Have you considered ever maybe getting married sometime in the near future?"

I scrunch my nose in confusion. *Was that a marriage proposal?* "You don't have to dance around the topic. I've always been open to marriage for future me. Like in my thirties."

He drops his hands. "Okay, I can wait."

I smile. "But that was before I met you."

He smiles widely and pulls a ring box from a high shelf in the cabinet. The advantage of his height—he can hide stuff from me on high shelves. My heart races.

Mom appears in the kitchen out of nowhere. "Wait! We want pictures of the proposal."

Dad pokes his head in the kitchen too, grinning.

Two things hit me at once. Cal cleared this with my parents ahead of time, and I'm getting married to the love of my life!

We move things into the living room. Dad turns off the music and barks, "Quiet! Big moment coming up for Mackenzie and Cal." The room quiets instantly.

Everyone pulls their phones out for pics and probably video too. I don't mind. It's all family.

Cal takes both my hands in his and drops to one knee. "Mackenzie Campbell, I will love you for all of my life and will do everything in my power to be your partner in all things, to support your dreams, to share your joy and your sorrows. I never knew how much I could love someone until I met you." His eyes water from unshed tears. "I will love you forever, always in my heart."

Oh God, I'm going to cry. He talks now about keeping love in his heart after loss, and it helps him to deal with the fear of losing me. "Always in my heart, Cal." Tears flow freely down my cheeks.

His eyes leak tears now too. "Will you marry me?"

I nod, barely able to speak over the lump in my throat. "Yes." He slides the diamond ring on my finger, stands, and gathers me into his arms, hugging me tight.

"Congratulations!" Mom exclaims, wiping tears.

"Champagne!" Dad croaks.

After we've recovered from our teary emotional moment, Mom and Dad make a toast.

Mom holds up her champagne glass. "I knew I'd be planning your wedding soon!" she crows triumphantly.

Cal smiles and takes my hand. I shake my head at her.

Mom smiles. "And, yes, I was doing a teensy bit of matchmaking when I told you to stay away from Cal. And I'm not sorry."

"You didn't fool me for a moment," I declare. "Okay, maybe a moment."

"Reverse matchmaking is still matchmaking," Dad says to Mom sternly. "I'd be mad if Mackenzie weren't so happy." He turns to us. "I hope you'll both be very happy and have a long life together. To Cal and Mackenzie!"

Everyone drinks to that. After lots of congratulations from everyone, the music starts again. Mom directs clearing some furniture so the dancing can begin.

Harper pulls me aside. "Any chance I can stay in the garage for a while?"

"Why?" She's been staying at her parents' house until she finds a house of her own. Our detached garage was previously converted to an office space for Harper, fully wired and with heating and cooling. No kitchen or bathroom, though. It's more of a storage space now.

Nathan joins us. "You want to live in a garage?"

Harper ignores him and looks at Cal. "If it's okay with you. I know you're newly engaged and all that. You wouldn't even know I was there."

"Fine by me," Cal says.

"Why would you want to live there when you've got your parents' huge house?" I ask.

Harper sighs. "Because Dad's so happy to have one of his kids home that he's reinstituted *daily* family dinners and weekend movie nights. He wants to know the best and worst part of my day, every day, like our family convos when I was ten years old. It's stifling."

I smile. Uncle Jake has become sentimental now that he and Aunt Claire have been empty nesters for a few years. "Aww, I think it's cute."

Harper grimaces. "He sings 'We're a Family' every time we come to the table. It's a *Sesame Street* song, Mac."

We all laugh except Harper. "Not funny," she mumbles.

"Maybe it's time to go house hunting," I say.

"No. I want to save up more before I house hunt. Maybe next year."

I'm about to say it's okay when Nathan pipes up, "You can stay with me."

Harper's eyes widen. "You want me to move into your place?"

"I have an apartment over the garage," he says. "The guy who lived there moved out a few months ago. I'll let you stay rent-free so you can keep saving for your dream house."

"What is your dream house anyway?" I ask.

Harper doesn't answer. She and Nathan are too busy staring at each other. "Why?"

He shrugs. "Helping an old friend out. I keep things in good condition, and I'm only a call away if something needs fixing." Nathan worked construction jobs in the summer during college and can do handyman stuff. That's right, the trust-fund baby likes to work with his hands.

She tilts her head, studying him like she's trying to figure out his angle.

Nathan gestures toward her. "I'd feel better knowing someone was around to keep an eye on the place since I'm away for jobs a lot, and you could, uh, bring in the mail and water the plants."

He's not away for jobs that much, mostly local stuff. Usually Owen takes the jobs in LA, and his wife, Shayla, goes with him to take meetings. Nathan is holding out the olive branch of peace between them, but Harper focuses on completely the wrong thing.

"You keep plants alive?" Harper asks.

He gives her a sour look. "Is that a yes?"

"Let me think about it."

He inclines his head. "You have until midnight."

"Why?"

"Because then I put the rental back on the market."

She crosses her arms. "So you have this apartment waiting, and suddenly it has to be filled right away?"

"Yes." He crosses his arms, mirroring her stance. "And maybe I'm trying to do something nice for you because I'm tired of you thinking I'm death to every party. Whatever was in the past is water under the bridge."

She lifts her chin. "Past never bothered me a bit."

"Good."

"Fine. I'll get the keys from you tomorrow."

They stare at each other. I tiptoe away, and Cal follows.

Once we're out of hearing range, Cal asks, "Was that their version of flirting?"

"That was a truce. It's good. This falling-out of theirs has gone on long enough."

He grins. "Is this like that movie where she says she hates him, but she secretly loves him?"

I smile widely. "Look at you with the romcom movie references. And I thought you fell asleep during that one." I loop my arms around his neck and kiss him. I only started loving romance once I experienced it for myself. In fact, I'm the newest romance reader in the Happy Endings Book Club. What a fun group. There's nothing better than swooning together over true love.

He wraps his arms around my waist. "I take an interest in everything you love because I love you so much I'm bursting with it." He mimes his heart exploding.

My heart melts. Still, I like to tease Cal about his newly blossoming sense of romance.

"Next thing you're going to be writing me love poems," I say.

"Now you're being ridiculous. You're the one who's going to be writing me love sonnets and sending me flowers."

We smile at each other. He's still in awe that I got him flowers. I like that I was the first person to do that for him.

And then our song starts playing, the slow song we

danced to when we first met, Etta James's "At Last." So fitting. At last we found each other.

We join the party, where several couples are already dancing. I look into his soulful eyes with all the love in my heart, surrounded by family and friends. Now the fun part really begins.

Don't miss the next book in the series, *The Tempting Part*, where Harper takes Nathan up on his offer of a free apartment, no strings attached. But will she be able to resist temptation when her sworn frenemy delivers such personal handyman service?

Sign up for my newsletter to be emailed when *The Tempting Part* releases. https://www.kyliegilmore.com/newsletter

P.S. Check out where Hailey and Josh's story began in the free book *Hidden Hollywood*.

ALSO BY KYLIE GILMORE

Not My Romeo (Book 6)

Rev Me Up (Book 7)

An Ambitious Engagement (Book 8)

Clutch Player (Book 9)

A Tempting Friendship (Book 10)

Clover Park Bride: Nico and Lily's Wedding

A Valentine's Day Gift (Book 11)

Maggie Meets Her Match (Book 12)

The Clover Park Charmers series <<sweet and sexy charmers!

Almost Over It (Book 1)

Almost Married (Book 2)

Almost Fate (Book 3)

Almost in Love (Book 4)

Almost Romance (Book 5)

Almost Hitched (Book 6)

The Rourkes Series <<swoonworthy princes and kickass princesses!

Royal Catch (Book 1)

Royal Hottie (Book 2)

Royal Darling (Book 3)

Royal Charmer (Book 4)

Royal Player (Book 5)

Royal Shark (Book 6)

Rogue Prince (Book 7)

Rogue Gentleman (Book 8)

Rogue Rascal (Book 9)

Rogue Angel (Book 10)

Rogue Devil (Book 11)

Rogue Beast (Book 12)

Unleashed Romance <<steamy romcoms with dogs!

Fetching (Book 1)

Dashing (Book 2)

Sporting (Book 3)

Toying (Book 4)

Blazing (Book 5)

Chasing (Book 6)

Daring (Book 7)

Leading (Book 8)

Racing (Book 9)

Loving (Book 10)

Check out my website for the most up-to-date list of my books:
kyliegilmore.com/books

ABOUT THE AUTHOR

Kylie Gilmore is the *USA Today* bestselling author of over fifty humorous contemporary romances. Her series include Happy Endings in Clover Park, Unleashed Romance, the Rourkes, the Happy Endings Book Club, Clover Park, and Clover Park Charmers. With more than three million downloads of her books, readers all over the world love escaping into her hilarious feel-good romances featuring strong bonds with family, friends, and community.

Kylie lives in New York with her family. When she's not writing, reading hot romance, or dutifully taking notes at writing conferences, you can find her happily crafting what will surely be future family heirlooms.

Sign up for Kylie's Newsletter and get a FREE book! kyliegilmore.com/newsletter

For more fun stuff check out Kylie's website https://www.kyliegilmore.com.